About the Author

Kathleen Harryman lives in York, with her husband and two daughters, and family dog and cat.

After attending writing groups, Kathleen was inspired to write her own book based around the city where she lives. Stories run through Kathleen's head whilst out walking the family dog. The miles disappear and are replaced with stories that are then brought to life in print. Writing is a natural part of Kathleen, and she enjoys watching the characters come to life.

For Mum, thanks for believing.

Kathleen Harryman

THE OTHER SIDE OF THE LOOKING GLASS

AUSTIN MACAULEY PUBLISHERS™

LONDON • CAMBRIDGE • NEW YORK • SHARJAH

A CIP catalogue record for this title is available from the British Library.

ISBN 9781785543425 (Paperback)
ISBN 9781785543432 (Hardback)
ISBN 9781785543449 (E-Book)

www.austinmacauley.com

First Published (2016)
Austin Macauley Publishers Ltd.
25 Canada Square
Canary Wharf
London
E14 5LQ

Acknowledgments

I would like to thank Annette Longman – Chief Editor, Hayley Knight – Senior Editor, Walter Stephenson – Editor, and everyone else at Austin Macauley Publishers, without you none of this would have been possible. Thanks for taking a chance in me.

I would also like to say a special thank you to my two girls for being patient when Mummy is trying to write a story, and to Stephen, my husband, for spending afternoons in the cold watching our girls playing in the park, trying to give me a quiet place to work. You're a diamond.

June Chappell – Mum, thanks for being my critic and giving me the confidence and belief to make me keep going; it's a hard road sometimes.

Neville Chappell – Dad, thankfully I inherited your stubbornness; it's kept me going when there have been times I thought I would never get there.

Lillian – sorry I kept you up all night; your comments gave me a real boost, thank you.

Lastly, I would like to thank you the reader, if it were not for you who would I share my stories with?

Chapter One

Kate

I woke to the clinical smell of detergent.

I lay staring at the tiled white ceiling for a while, allowing my brain to catch up with what my other senses were trying to tell me. The sun glaring through the window to my right told me that it was daytime. A chair sat next to a small white nightstand. Some sunflowers sat in a vase on top of the unit. I smiled; I liked sunflowers.

An irritating beep-beep sounded near my left ear, which brought my attention to the fact that my left hand hurt. I lifted my head slightly to find wires littering my body. I quickly dropped my head back down on the pillow and took stock of what the wires and the beeping meant.

I let out a hard sigh.

I hate hospitals, but then name me a patient that likes them. There's that clinical smell for one, and secondly, they're filled with sick people; for obvious reasons. I did not put myself in the category of '*sick people*'.

This hospital did smell nicer than the ones I had stayed in before. Now, that brought another thought rattling round my brain. Had I been in a hospital before? Well it must appear so, or I wouldn't have had the thought in the first place. The problem was that the more I thought about things, about me, my life, the more I found that all that there was, was an empty space.

My life was a blank.

I couldn't even remember how old I was. What I looked like? What colour my eyes were? Did I have a favourite colour?

Panic seized me.

I swallowed it down, after all it wouldn't do me any good, and, anyway, why expend energy I didn't have.

I looked down at my hands. I was definitely of a certain age, not a child, or a teenager, or even a very young woman. Maybe I was thirty; thirty sounded like a good age. Now why would I think that? I needed a mirror; maybe looking at my reflection would bring some clarity.

I went to move my legs and became aware of something lying between them. I lifted the sheets, and came to the conclusion I couldn't really see anything while I was laid flat. Pushing myself up to a sitting position didn't really suit my heavy limbs, and would expend energy I simply didn't feel I had. Now, if I remembered rightly (and here was me having another one of those thoughts that I couldn't place to a particular moment in my life), hospital beds had these little switches to move the bed, and patient to a sitting position. I moved my hand feeling round the side of the bed. Not this side, hmm, better try the other side, and there it was. I pressed the button, and the bed began to lift upward until I was in a slightly elevated position. Now I'd accomplished such a major feat, I was ready to have a better look at what was between my legs. Hmm, a pale pink tube. Well, what on earth was a pale pink tube doing there? It seemed to disappear off to my right, so I moved slightly, peering over to the right side of the bed, and that's when I saw the bag of wee. Well, wasn't that just dandy. I felt disgusted at the thought, but you have to look at things from a brighter angle at some point, and the only one I could think of right now, was that at least the wee was in the bag, and not soaking the bed.

OK, so what did all this tell me?

For one, I'd been here sometime; the bag was definitely reaching full capacity. Second, no one expected me to be bouncing out bed anytime soon. That wasn't a pleasant thought. Now I was awake I wanted out of this bed, down the hall, and out the front door.

I laid my head back against the pillow; a dull throb was beginning to set in my head. I raised my right hand (as the left one had the needle stuck in it, and was beginning to hurt like a bitch), and placed it on my head. Hmm, now why would I be wearing a hat?

Hang on!

I was in hospital, with needles, wires and tubes stuck in me, and coming out of certain places I didn't really care to think about. That was no hat on top of my head. *Nope*, it had to be a bandage.

Next question.

What had happened to me?

I rattled the thought round my brain for a while and gave up. No memory existed. *Breathe deep,* I told myself as my heart began hammering. I just needed something to jog my memory; that was all. Panicking was only going to make my head hurt more than it was starting to do already.

The door to the room opened, and I turned my head in that direction. That's when another thought struck me, I was in a room all on my own. Did I have money? These things weren't cheap.

Or worse, was I really that sick to warrant such a luxury as my own room? Now that was a perplexing thought, so I decided not to dwell on it.

"Do you have a mirror?" The woman looked at me a little startled. From her attire, I guessed she was the nurse tasked with checking on me and my vitals.

Her very pink hair was wound up on top of her head, which was littered with pins that weren't doing a very good job. From the tired look on her face I'd say she was coming to the end of her shift. Her overall was pale blue and did nothing for her figure, which was pear in shape. It didn't help that she was five foot nothing, and obviously liked to eat more than she spent in energy.

"You're awake." Her big blue eyes widened in surprise.

Hmm, she wasn't so clever for a nurse. Maybe I didn't have money after all. I didn't feel as though I was going to get the best type of treatment from her, after all who has pink hair in their fifties?

"I'll go get the doctor." And with that she was gone, and I was alone, without a mirror, I might add. I was starting to feel annoyed; after all, I didn't feel that asking for a mirror was a hard task. Obviously, it was.

The longer I laid here on my own, unable to move, and without my simple request for a mirror, the grumpier I could feel myself becoming. Maybe I was one of those *'awful patients'* people often spoke about.

I looked down at my left hand. Hmm, that didn't look right. I placed my right hand next to my left and compared the two. My left hand was twice as big as the other one. Had my hands always been like this? *Of course, they bloody hadn't!* I eyed the needle, which allowed the hydration fluid to enter my body. That was the culprit, I'd wager everything I had on it.

The door opened again and a man in a white coat walked in, followed by the *nurse.* The doctor smiled at me. It was a nice warm smile that even reached his caramel eyes. His face was smoothly shaven, probably just starting his shift, *the lucky boy*. His black hair had threads of white running through it; he reminded me of George Clooney, in a less rugged way, and more of a man used to working long hours, over too many days. The stripy purple shirt stood out against the white of his coat, and his black trousers looked a little on the short side. Had they always been like that, or were they the result of a washing disaster? I'd had more than a few of those in my time.

Hmm, so I wasn't rich then, if I were rich I'd have someone else doing my laundry for me.

I looked back at the doctor; he reached the six-foot mark, towering over the nurse, his tanned skin making the paleness of the nurse's stand out.

"It's good to see you awake, Mrs Thornton." His voice was deep and his words nicely pronounced. His deep twang appealed to me for whatever reason.

Mrs Thornton, was that really my name? I'd have questioned if he was talking to me, but as I was the only patient in the room, the possibilities of it being someone else were extremely limited.

"Do you have a mirror?" I could see from the way his eyebrows shot into the blackness of his hairline that my question had surprised him.

I'd wager everything I had again, that he had expected me to ask the typical question of where I was. Well, it was bloody obvious to me where I was. I was in a hospital. The question of where the hospital was didn't much matter, because it wouldn't tell me anything about me. A mirror just might.

"Nurse would you get Mrs Thornton a mirror." The nurse gave the doctor an adoring look, and turned around and walked back out the door.

I choose for the purpose of now, to ignore the fact that I was obviously married. There was no ring on my left hand.

I'd have noticed that when I was checking its bloated size. Maybe I was a widow or divorced. *Great*; well, if that was the case maybe forgetting my past life might not be such a bad thing. Who was I kidding; the not knowing about me was quickly eating away at me. I thought about the mirror that the nurse was getting and smiled to myself; soon I'd get a look at myself, and questions were going to be answered.

The doctor came around to the foot of the bed and started filling in some sheets of paper on a clipboard, looking occasionally at the data the machines were chunking out.

The door opened again and my smile grew bigger, only to come crashing down at the corners, as a man wearing a well cut dark grey suit came running in to the room. His dark chocolate brown hair fell forward as he raced over to my bed. I didn't really get much of a chance to get a good look at him; as he came running at me, like a fruit bat spying a grape for the first time. Had I been able to, I would have leaped off the bed and shut myself in the bathroom, which lay to the left of wall in front of me. As it was I had no alternative but to brace myself for whatever the man had in mind. Given that there was a doctor present I thought, mistakenly, that I'd be OK.

Two things happened to me at once.

Firstly, the man in the nice suit caught the needle in my left hand, and pain shot down my hand and up my arm, making me scream out. Secondly, taking no notice of my pain filled scream, I was forcefully pressed against the man's chest. At one point, I thought he was going to suffocate me. Being suffocated by Armani might not be the worse way to go, still I was hoping for a more uneventful passing, like dying in my sleep at a very old age.

"*Mr Thornton! Mr Thornton!*" I could hear the doctor shouting from the confines of the suit jacket.

Mr Thornton? Was this my husband? If so, I guess I wasn't divorced or widowed. I wasn't so sure how I felt about that now having said husband here.

"S-s-sorry," my husband stammered. One thing I did notice from that one word was that he was very well spoken, toffee in the mouth well spoken. I didn't really care for the underlying tones to his voice, he sounded very insincere.

My husband stepped back a little; his hand went for my left hand. Thankfully, I managed to move it before he got to it. I saw his frown; he didn't like that. That bothered me. Maybe I was being judgmental, because I couldn't remember him. He was a very nice-looking fellow as far as total strangers went. He just didn't seem like my type though. That was a puzzling thought. At just under six-foot with a medium frame, sharp blue eyes in a thin hawkish face, he just didn't feel like the sort of guy I'd have married. Hmm, so if my husband wasn't my type then who was? Maybe it was his clean-shaven baby soft face, or the fake tan that had an unfortunate orange glow to it that was putting me off.

If I weren't divorced, maybe I had been thinking about it?

My head hit my pillow and I stared at the white wall in front of me, well this was awkward. My husband began to stare at me, eyes narrowing a little at the corners. I began to realise that my silence was not helping the situation.

"My hand hurts, and it's all swollen," I said, breaking the silence, diverting the attention away from my face. My husband looked down at my hand. I put my right hand next to it, making my point.

"Doctor?" It's strange how some people can make one word sound like a scolding. My husband was very use to getting his own way.

The doctor reacted to the harshness in my husband's voice; money can do that. And my husband had money. He oozed the stuff, right down to the stitching on his very expensive suit, to the glint of gold from his Rolex watch. And yet I wasn't impressed. I wasn't shallow then. Was that a good thing?

Luckily for all concerned the nurse chose that moment to enter the room. The doctor reacted to her presence, looking at my husband. "Why don't you get a coffee Mr Thornton, while we make your wife more comfortable?" If that meant taking the needle out of my left hand, removing the pale pink tube from between my legs, and getting rid of all the machinery, plus getting my mirror, then I was all for it.

My husband gave the doctor an assessing look. I couldn't quite work out what the look meant. It's not like I was going to get up and run off. Wow, where had that come from? Why would I want to run away?

"My head hurts," I croaked.

The doctor nodded at the nurse, and with a skill her profession required, she ushered my husband out the door and drew the curtain, blocking out the rest of the room.

"Why can't I remember him?" I pointed a finger at the door now hidden by the curtain.

"Hmmm, well, better not to worry about that for now. Let's just get you comfortable. Nurse?" I heard the door to my room open and the nurse came running through the curtain. Was the doctor psychic? Or was it just good timing?

With a speed of someone who had done this one too many times, the tube was removed from between my legs and my vitals checked. The needle from my left hand removed and the wires disappeared. It felt good to have my body back under my control. The nurse and doctor muttered between themselves. I would have interrupted them, but thought better of it; I'd get my chance later to ask my questions. I was obviously a patient person, and that surprised me, and made me happy at the same time.

It's quite strange getting to know yourself; I kept wondering what else I might learn.

"So why can't I remember anything?" I asked as soon as everything was done and the curtain drawn back.

I obviously wasn't that patient.

The doctor stood back and gave me a considering look. "What can you remember?"

I thought about this for a brief second; as my head was filled with nothing, it didn't take too long. "Nothing, I woke up here, and that's about it."

"I see." I was glad one of us saw something. "It's probably due to your head injury." From my blank look and the way my hand flew up to my head, the doctor would be right in thinking the head injury took me by surprise. Even though I'd discovered the bandage on waking, I hadn't made the connection between the bandage and a head injury. "You fell down some stairs."

I fell down some stairs! Really, was I that clumsy? I must have gone with some speed to wind up here, and head first by the looks of it. Well, I guess that explained the hospital and the bandage, but it didn't explain why I couldn't remember anything. "When will I be able to remember?"

"We'll run some tests." I got the feeling that the doctor mentioned this to make me feel better, with the added benefit of shutting me up.

"Here," the nurse handed me a small looking glass.

That got my attention.

I stared at the person in the reflection. I was quite a beauty. I say this not in a vain way, but as someone looking at another person; accepting and appreciating what they saw. Thick long black lashes framed the soft almond shape of my emerald green eyes, which burnt bright against the soft creamy caramel of my skin. Even with a bandage wrapped round the top of my head, my hair fell to my waist like black silk, framing my face. I touched my cheek running a thin graceful finger along my high cheek bone. Exotic, that's how I'd describe myself. I couldn't stop looking at the stranger in the mirror; she was a mystery to me, a puzzle to be put together piece by piece. One I wanted to find out about, after all this was me, and not some stranger. I couldn't just walk through the rest of my life not knowing who I truly was. No, I had to start remembering something, anything.

"Don't try to push yourself into remembering. The more you do, the harder it will be." The doctor's voice was soft, comforting. No wonder the nurse was smitten with him, as far as bedside manners went, it would be fair to say he excelled at it.

I put down the mirror. "Why can't I remember?" I asked again.

The doctor sighed, "Until we run more tests I'm not really able to answer that question."

I did something that surprised me, I burst into tears. My body shook as I sobbed, small hiccups falling from my lips. I wasn't bothered about being in hospital, nor did it bother me as to the reason why I'd ended up here. No, what bothered me was the not knowing about my life, about me. My lack of memory disturbed me more than waking up in hospital, or the injuries I had sustained.

Outside the door to my room stood a man I had no memory of, and didn't think I liked very much; and yet he seemed to care about me. Enough to be here when I woke. Obviously, it could have been a coincidence that he'd been here the moment I'd woken up. As soon as the thought came into my head, it served to illustrate my dislike for him. Maybe it had something to do with the shiftiness that seemed to ooze off him. My husband was shifty, that was it. There was something about him that said to me *'can't- be-trusted'*. Then again, if he was rich, there was going to be an air of confidence, and shiftiness about him. Not that I had anything against rich people. Or, did I? I didn't know, because I couldn't remember. Tears flowed down my cheeks, as I gave a loud sniff. I hated feeling like this.

How could I possibly trust someone I didn't know? Maybe that was the problem. My husband could be one of those people that you were better for knowing.

The nurse placed a comforting arm around my shoulders making small shushing noises. She was obviously well versed in comforting, and practical with it. As one arm snaked around my shoulders, in her other hand was a tissue, which she pressed into my empty hands. I blew my nose.

The door opened and my husband walked in. I needed to know what his name was, because I couldn't go on calling him my husband. Maybe if I knew his name, I might feel friendlier towards him.

"I can't remember anything." I sobbed. My husband looked at me.

"It could be that your wife may be suffering from amnesia, but we'll need to run some more tests first," the doctor injected.

More tears fell down my cheek. My husband took over from the nurse and snuck an arm around my shoulders, softly pressing me against his chest. He smelt nice, expensive nice. Despite this, it took a lot of willpower not pull away from the man I was supposedly married to.

"I don't know your name," I cried into the softness of his jacket.

"Liam." He had a shifty name too. Gosh, I was having really horrible thoughts. I think that even if he'd been called John or Luke, or George, or Sam, I would have still thought the same thing. Most unfair, I know.

"The doctor says I fell down some stairs," I croaked into the jacket. I gave a big sniff, and used the excuse of blowing my nose to subtly move away slightly from him.

Liam looked down at me. "You can't remember anything?" The tone in his voice told me he knew more than he was letting on.

21

"Not a thing." I stared at him, meeting those sharp blue eyes.

"You fell down the stairs at the multi-storey car park in York at the Coppergate Centre." His eyes softened. "We were supposed to meet for coffee, and you were running late. I told you not to rush, but you know how you hate being late." Nope, I didn't, because I didn't have a memory. "A man tried to get your handbag as you were running down the stairs. I just don't understand why you just didn't let him have it."

"*I was mugged?*" I asked, amazed.

"Yes." Liam gave me another one of his long stares.

"Were you there?" From the look on his face I'd say he didn't like the question.

"No, not when it happened."

My body went limp and I sagged against Liam, only because he had yet to remove his arm from my shoulders. "I'm tired," I said more to myself than anyone else.

"Yes, of course. Mr Thornton, I am sure you must have some questions." I smiled at the doctor, as he moved towards the door. I had to hand it to him, because in that one sentence, he hadn't left Liam much choice but to tag along behind him.

"Of course," Liam said.

I tried not to shrink back when Liam bent and kissed my cheek.

My unease must have shown because his blue eyes narrowed in on me. "Sorry, it's just that you're a stranger to me. I mean, not a stranger, obviously. I just can't remember you." I was babbling.

He gave me a long look but nodded his head. I was grateful for the small bit of understanding he showed me. I had to admit, even to myself, that it couldn't be easy for him either. Here I was, his wife, the person he had spent lord knows how many years being married to, and I was treating him like little more than a stranger.

The nurse gave me another once over before leaving the room, and then I was alone again. My eyes felt heavy and before I knew it sleep claimed me.

Chapter Two

Jessica

"Are you sure this is going to work?" I looked at Charles. His hazel eyes softened at my unease. He pushed himself away from his desk, and stepped towards me. His ink black hair fell to the collar of his white coat. His golden tanned skin stood out against the stark white fabric of his doctor's coat, as I liked to call it, though with Charles being a consultant, I guess the name doctor could be considered an insult. Charles was built like a rugby player. Broad shoulders, and thick muscle on a six-foot-six frame. He made me feel safe, something I hadn't felt for such an awfully long time. The thought of what we were doing made me nervous, but we had gone too far to stop now.

"He trusts me Jess; he'll never suspect a thing." Charles raised his hand and gently pushed back my long silky black hair.

"But telling him I've got cancer and I'm dying seems so wrong somehow." The lies were beginning to eat away at me; the severity of the lie made me feel uncomfortable.

"It's the only way he's ever going to let you go." I nodded my head in agreement. I was desperate, and I mean desperate, to get away from my husband. I couldn't even tell you why I'd married him. It had never been about love, not for either of us. I thought about Liam and those early years. He'd always treated me nice, buying me things, making sure that I had everything I needed. When you have nothing, and aren't used to having anything, then it's easy to be overwhelmed when someone wants to shower you with gifts. And that's what Liam had done. I'd never stopped to think about what I was getting myself into. Liam, well he got what he wanted, a wife that stood out from the crowd, beautiful and exotic, and Liam liked the exotic.

I looked at my reflection through the window. Darkness had set in, turning the glass from window to mirror. Almond-shaped emerald green eyes stared back at me; my long black silky hair fell gracefully down my back. I ran a delicate hand through the thickness of my mane of hair. I was small boned, as people liked to say, or just plain skinny. I had curves in the right places, just not overly pronounced; they didn't say *come-on-boys*, so much as *you- can't-afford-this-one*.

I had never thought of myself as beautiful until I'd met Liam. He'd taken me out, showed me how to dress, and removed the rough edges, until all that was left was the polish and shine of sophistication. My pale pink Armani cropped trousers hugged my slim thighs, while the white silk shirt nipped in at my narrow waist and accentuated my small breasts. The padded push um' up bra probably helped. These pale colours set off the natural creamy caramel tones of my skin. Liam never allowed me to wear a pair of ripped jeans, or lounge around the house in joggy bottoms and a scruffy t-shirt that had some silly slogan written across it. Liam believed in looking your best *always*; I even had to sleep with a trace of light makeup.

People stared at Liam and me when we went out; we were, after all, impeccably dressed. The men would slap him on the back, and tell him how lucky he was to have such a rare beauty for a wife, as though I was some object that Liam had picked up from a high-end store. Liam just soaked it up, and me, well, I'd grown up fast. I'd soon learnt that there was more to life than what money could buy. Charles Cavendish had shown me what love meant, what it was about. And believe me, it had nothing to do with how I looked, but more about my personality, about the inner me.

I looked at Charles; my heart gave a little flutter. We'd never intended to fall in love. Charles, he was everything that Liam wasn't; easy to laugh, kind, caring and so much more. I traced a long delicate finger along his strong jaw line and smiled. His face lit up at my touch.

Charles took me into his arms. I slid my arms across his broad shoulders and wrapped them round his neck. My feet left the floor as he hugged me to him. I was only five-foot-two, and Charles had at least another foot and a bit on me. I breathed in his musky sent and felt safe. I felt loved.

"It's going to be OK," Charles breathed into my neck. I had to believe that it would be. Because if Liam ever found out about us, or what we had done, or were about to do, he would kill us both for sure.

The day I had become Mrs Thornton, was the day that Liam had taken possession of me. Liam bought and manipulated his way through life. I now knew that all I was, and all I would ever be, was yet another bauble to own and show off. One that Liam would never let go. No one played with Liam's toys, and what was his remained his, alone. Only death would free me, or in my case the faux pretence of cancer.

Not even Liam could control cancer.

It was a truly horrible thing that Charles and I were doing, but as I said, we were desperate. I apologised to all those suffering from the disease, and those that had died. To the families that had had their worlds broken apart by cancer.

Liam was my cancer, I wanted rid, I wanted so much to live and be happy.

I'd been coming here to Charles' clinic for a while now. It's where we met to spend time together, to be close to each other, without causing suspicion. Our plan was a simple one; after all it's the simple ones that seemed to work the best.

Charles had handed his notice in at the clinic where he worked, six months ago and had stayed on to 'treat' me as a favour to Liam. I had arranged to go away somewhere peaceful to die, and that was when Charles and I would finally be together.

I had recently opened an account in the name of Jessica Ripley, which is why Charles called me Jess rather than Kate. Charles had arranged the new identify for me, after all, I couldn't go around using the name Kate Thornton. It wouldn't take a genius to track me down, should Liam ever get suspicious. And Liam was not the trusting type, even if Charles thought that it was different with him. They'd been friends since senior school, and Charles had helped Liam out of a couple of scrapes when he was much younger, before the icy threads of greed and fortune had grasped hold of Liam.

I could still remember Liam's reaction when I'd told him about the cancer. I'd thought he was going to combust on the spot. He must have thought better of it, because instead he had grabbed me by the arm, thrown me into his Bentley, and driven like hell itself was after us, straight to the clinic, and to Charles. Liam had then demanded that Charles do something.

We'd been ready for this, and Charles and whipped out some X-rays that belonged to someone else, and shown Liam how bad things really were. I had closed by eyes and prayed for forgiveness when those X-rays had lit up. Over and over again I had reminded myself that this was the only way. Charles had caught my despair, and had pulled out a chair and made me sit down, his eyes had told me how much he'd wanted to take me into his arms, to comfort me and tell me we were doing the right thing. But Liam was there, and we

27

couldn't blow things, not now, otherwise this would all be for nothing, and Liam would take out his revenge on us both.

It had taken Liam two hours before he actually calmed down. I could almost see his brain ticking over, calculating his next move. Having a sick wife was not what Liam wanted; sympathy was not an emotion that he cared to have directed his way. I'd got to know Liam pretty well during our marriage. I'd taken the time to learn his tells and try and work out the way that his devious brain ticked. Too bad Liam had never taken the time to learn more about me. Otherwise, he might have seen the small lines of worry that had crept along my brow, or the nervous way that my fingers had twitched in my lap.

Charles had noticed.

I saw his hazel eyes stray to my twitching fingers on more than one occasion.

"So how long has she got?" The distain in Liam's voice had been hard to miss.

"About six months, it's hard to for sure. Charles had answered for me.

"Six months, hmm I don't suppose with such a short time span there's any point in prolonging the evitable with more treatment. The last thing I need is for your hair to be dropping out, or you being sick." That was Liam, caring to the last.

Charles couldn't help the way his jaw had dropped down to his chest at Liam's words. I'd been ready for them. Even as prepared as I was, it was still a bit of a kick in the teeth to be tossed aside by my own husband, in such a callous manner.

"Liam," Charles just hadn't been able to keep quiet. "Kate's your wife not some…"

"And now she'll soon be dead," Liam bit out.

Charles had snapped his jaw shut and said nothing else. "I'll leave you to make the necessary arrangements. Let me know the final bill, and I'll wire the money over to you." With that Liam had left, without me.

You would have thought that after that day, I would be happier about what Charles and I were doing; I was certainly more resigned to it. I just wish there had been some way to do this without such a terrible lie.

Chapter Three

Liam

I couldn't believe what the bitch had done to me.

I sat outside the Judge's Lodging, which was situated near the post office in the heart of York's city centre, the sun beating down on my grey Armani suit. I swirled my second gin and tonic round the glass. It felt like the weather was having a good laugh at my expense. I couldn't see anything to be bright about.

I had taken the bitch in, made her what she was today. I'd even forgiven her for her middle-class background. If I had left her with her drug-infested aunt she would probably be dead by now. Just like her parents, and her adoptive parents were. I tapped the file in front of me. I never did anything without first getting every scrap of information I could, and Kate had not been an exception. If you made just one exception then you were going to fail, and I was no failure. The amount of money I had made over the years was proof of that.

I opened the file and reread the information again. Kate's parents had died in a house fire when she was six. Luckily, Kate and her sister had been saved. This had led to them being adopted, as their aunt on her mother's side hadn't wanted them at the time. That was until their adoptive parents had died in a car crash a year later, and they'd both been taken in by their aunt. Apparently, she had changed her mind, about her responsibility towards her nieces.

Death seemed to follow Kate around.

I should have taken that into consideration, I chastised myself silently, as I watched the ice swirl round the glass in my hand. Maybe some would think it fitting that now death was about to claim her. I didn't, because no one, *no one*, left me until I wanted them to.

Kate, well the bitch had found a way to leave me.

I'd known Kate hadn't been happy for a while. What did I care? If the bitch couldn't be satisfied with her lot, that was her fault, it had nothing to do with me. I had showered that bitch with gifts, given her a life that most envied. And the bitch had to get cancer.

The information in front of me was somewhat hazy when Kate and her sister had been taken in by their aunt, after the death of their adoptive parents. The fact that Kate's sister seemed to disappear during the stay with the aunt, I'd say was of some concern, but then if the authorities hadn't been able to see what was going on in that house, then you couldn't blame them for losing sight of a child.

I downed the rest of my drink and stared at the people around me, discounting them. That's when I saw Kate, hanging on some man's arm, smiling and looking oh-so-happy, and very well. My top lip curled in distaste, as I took note of what she was wearing. Faded jeans that had seen much better days, and a pale pink t-shirt that had some logo on that was supposed to make you smile, of which, had the opposite effect on me. I was beyond such simplistic novelty things. These clothes were high street trash, not the quality designer items I liked Kate to wear.

The more I stared at her the angrier I became.

The bitch was having an affair!

I didn't recognise the man, but I'd make sure that this was the last time he ever got to see the sun; by tomorrow he'd be dead. I couldn't wait to inflict the pain of this man's death on Kate. That would teach her to stray. It was as well that she herself was dying; still, it wouldn't hurt to beat some sense into her, make sure that she didn't make the same mistake again, for however long she had to live.

My phone took that moment to ring. I looked down at it considering if I was going to answer it, or not. It was Kate. My head snapped up; the woman in front of me didn't have a mobile phone in her hand. In fact, she was now too busy kissing the man with her, to care about a phone.

"Liam?" Kate's voice sounded in my ear.

"Not now," I ended the call, and started taking pictures of the mystery woman.

My brain started to go into overdrive; maybe I wasn't going to be beaten after all. I smiled and ordered another gin and tonic from the passing waiter. I flipped through the photos I'd taken on my phone. Had I not known any better, I'd have said that the woman was Kate. That's when everything snapped into place.

Kate's sister was her twin, *her identical twin.*

The waiter came back with my gin and tonic. I threw a tenner in his direction and waved him off, and called Pete Townend.

"I've sent you a photo. Maybe you'd like to explain why you failed to tell me that Kate's sister wasn't just her sister, *but* her twin, *her identical twin.*" I smiled, because Pete was going to do me one hell of an assignment.

No one fed me incorrect information without paying the price, and Pete was about to discover what that price was going to be. With Charles leaving to go live in some remote place in Scotland, there was nobody to stop me.

The phone echoed with the urgent fumbling's of a man not quite prepared to accept their fate. My lips thinned. "Well I haven't got all day. Frankly, I think I've waited long enough. How many years is it since you compiled the information on Kate for me?" I didn't wait for Pete to answer. "I'll tell you Pete, six years. *Six years*, and in that time, you never bothered to check the information that I paid you for was correct. You know I'm not a tolerant man, Pete. Tolerance is for fools, and I will not be treated like a fool."

"You didn't specify how far back to go. So, I only did a preliminary scan prior to Kate being taken in by her aunt. I did inform you about the sister. The aunt sold her to a couple who couldn't have children. You didn't seem that interested in the sister at the time."

I put down my glass with a thud, and hissed into the phone. "Pete, don't you ever try and weasel your way into thinking that this is my fault. It's not going to go away that easily.

"Whether I was interested in the sister at the time or not, is not the point, you should have done your job properly. You didn't and now you owe me."

"Mr Thornton…"

"I wouldn't go down that road if I were you, Pete. People like you are ten a penny. You have no living relatives, no wife, or children. It's fair to say that no one would miss you."

"Are you threatening me?" Pete sounded stunned. The poor man, was he really that stupid to think that he could just take my money and be free? Silly, silly, silly, man.

"No, Pete, I'm not threatening you. I am, however, telling you, that you have twenty-four hours to finish getting all the information on Kate and her sister. And by the way, just to clarify, when I say all the information, I mean even down to blood type. Meet me at my office, with the information, or you can kiss goodbye to your own existence. I hope I have made myself clear on this point."

"Yes," Pete bit out the word like someone was holding a gun to his head, ready to pull the trigger. The thought made me smile.

"Good, then I shall see you tomorrow at 10am sharp."

"But that's only sixteen hours away." At least Pete could do the maths.

"Then you had better get going." I hung up before Pete could stop spluttering.

I picked up my gin and tonic, and started to work out my options. First things first, I had to get the real Kate out the way. Killing her would be too easy, and why bother if she was going to die anyway. What I needed to do was get her to her final resting place sooner rather than later. Now, what was that saying, ah yes, treatment only prolonged the agony, so why bother?

I had thought about getting a second opinion, but Charles was my friend and sometimes you had to trust someone. It wasn't like this was a business deal, I wasn't going to make money from this, just lose it.

Now I'd seen the other Kate, well what would be the point in a second opinion?

What I needed to do now was get Kate far, far away from here.

Quickly.

Chapter Four

Jessica

"I just don't know Charles, something's wrong." I sat on the end of my bed looking out the patio door. The view across the lawn was breath-taking. The flowerbeds were in full bloom, producing a kaleidoscope of colour and scents. The grounds spread out for acres, fourteen of them to be precise. Two acres of which held manicured lawns and flower beds, the rest was divided up into pastures, and a small wooded area, where a stream ran through the middle, over rocks. A small wooden humpbacked bridge signalled the end of the property.

Jake McCloud, the gardener, was down there somewhere plucking out the weeds, and deadheading the flowers. Jake had worked for Liam, since forever. His arthritic body complained during the rainy days and cold mornings. Summer was Jake's best season, though his joints still complained, and his hands had begun to curl in on themselves. Jake was the happiest and most content person I had ever met. Jake Junior, as everyone called him, had been employed recently to pick up the slack, and do the jobs that Jake's body could no longer undertake.

Unfortunately for Jake Junior, the task of cutting the lawn with the sit-on lawn mower was one task that Jake's body allowed him do, with a lot of zeal. I opened the patio door and peered out. Leaning over the balcony, I saw Jake and Jake Junior, as the sit-on lawn mower roared to life. Jake Junior eyed the contraption as though it were a Ferrari. Jake barked out orders and Jake Junior gave the machine one last lingering look.

I'd miss this pair.

Jake, with his gnarled old body, thick snowy white hair on tanned leathery skin; eyes that shone golden brown, and the lines that scattered across his face like streets on a road map. Jake was the kindest person I had ever met.

Jake was also the only person I knew that Liam had never replaced once they had out lived their usefulness. Instead, Liam had employed Jake Junior, to help and assist Jake. I often wondered at the story that lay between them. Liam had refused to talk about it. Apparently, it was another one of those things that *wasn't any of my business*.

Jake Junior, with his splash of copper hair and thin lanky frame had brought happiness back into Jake's life. Jake, now had someone to pass on his knowledge to. Jake had never married. As a consequence, there weren't any kids in Jake's life to pass on his love of everything green, and brightly coloured. Jake Junior had sealed that gap well and truly closed.

I closed the door and walked back into the room.

"Liam has asked me if I can leave by the end of the week. I just don't get it, Charles. I know our news struck him hard, but even for Liam this is unusual behaviour. The only thing that Liam has asked me to do is leave my rings. Why would he do that? It's not like he needs the money." I took a breath. "Why does he want them? Liam never does anything without a reason. It's not that I want them, I'd never planned on taking my wedding or engagement ring with me." I was babbling again.

I took the rings off my finger for the first time since I had got married. The diamonds in both the wedding and engagement ring sparkled, sending light into the shadows. The platinum wedding band held a wealth of sizable princess cut diamonds that ran around the full length and width of the band. It complemented the six-carat clear princess cut diamond engagement ring. I didn't know the cost of the rings, but for the average person I reckon they would consist of a small fortune. A fortune that they would be able to ill afford, and would probably never earn in their entire lifetime.

"You're probably reading too much into it." Charles deep tones sounded in my ear.

"You could be right." I tried to relax, but it wasn't happening for me.

"What else has happened?" Charles asked. I could almost see him trying to work out Liam's reasons for asking for the rings.

"You mean, apart from the fact that Liam wants me out the house by Friday?"

"Well, I admit that was a bit of a shock. Liam came to see me yesterday, to ask me if I would drop you off to where ever it was that you were going to die. He wasn't even interested enough to ask where that might be." I could tell by the way he hesitated over the word die, that Charles found Liam's reaction difficult to understand. "You're probably right; Liam did seem a little off."

A little off! Alarm bells were sounding in my head at a rate so high they would be able to be heard over the top of a smoke alarm. "The sooner Friday comes, the better," I whispered in to the phone.

"There's only three more days to go, it won't be long now."

I flopped down onto the bed. "It sounds like an eternity." Charles laughed and I smiled into the phone.

"Can you meet for lunch?" I asked.

"How about an early tea?"

"That sounds good. I've got a few things to pick up ready for Friday. How about we meet at say 5ish?"

"5 sounds good, I'll book a table at The Star in the City."

"Charles, thanks for listening."

"Hey, there's no need for that, it's what I'm here for." Warmth filled my chest as my heart swelled in happiness, tiny rays of love, and a sense of belonging spread throughout my body. It was little things like this that made everything worth it. Tears stung the back of my eyes and I smiled into the phone.

"Love you," I whispered and hung up.

I placed the phone back on the hook, and looked round my room. The white wooden frame of the super-sized bed sat against the back wall taking up most of the space. Two matching white nightstands stood by each side of the bed. Opposite which, was a white wooden dressing table littered with creams, makeup, and perfumes. To the right of the bed opposite the patio doors lay two doors; one led to the en-suite bathroom, which housed a large walk-in shower, an oversized bath tub, sink, toilet and a cupboard, stocked with fluffy, high cotton count Egyptian towels. The other door led to a walk-in wardrobe / dressing room. This room was filled to breaking point with high class, high cost, designer labels. Armani, Stella McCartney, Gucci, Chanel, etcetera, hung on the racks, beneath them sat the matching shoes and handbags.

I wasn't planning on taking any of them with me.

I wanted normal.

To walk around in high street clothes that were made to be comfortable, and shoes that didn't nip at my toes, making my feet scream in pain.

Liam didn't care about comfort, or about my aching, sore feet.

Liam cared only about what I looked like, and making the right impression.

It was always business with Liam.

I couldn't wait to leave this all behind. As Charles had said, there were only three days to go. I sighed out my discomfort. Whatever Liam was up to, it soon wouldn't be my problem.

I picked up my small pale blue handbag from the end of the bed, and threw it over my shoulder, smoothing out my cream wide leg cotton trousers, and rearranging the pale powder blue silk blouse with its three-quarter sleeves. Pale blue wedge sandals finished off my outfit. I turned and looked at myself in the full-length mirror before I closed the dressing room door. My hair cascaded around my shoulders down to my waist. My creamy brown caramel skin glowed against the fine fabrics of my clothes.

Dare I say it, but I looked the picture of health. I could lie and say it's amazing the miracles that makeup can wield, but I wasn't sick, and despite my worries and concerns, I was very happy, giddy almost.

Closing the bedroom door, I made my way down the stairs. My footsteps echoed on the hard surface of the marble flooring. The staircase swept up from both sides of the hall, announcing its presence with grandeur and elegance. A large crystal chandelier hung from the ceiling, off which, smaller crystals tumbled down in tiny droplets.

Everything Liam did, he did with style, hiring the best there was to ensure that his expectations were met.

This house had been no exception to Liam's wants and desires.

The building was imposing with its white painted exterior and crisp stylish interior. Antiques littered the house like a statement of power and money. The house boasted fourteen bedrooms across two wings, all ensuite.

The very large ostentatious kitchen housed the top of the range gadgets that would be the envy of any chef. Not that Liam and I cooked; Liam employed people to do that, to the left of the kitchen was a large utility, and downstairs bathroom, with a walk-in shower. A sunroom, study, two living rooms, and a snug made up the lower floor. All the rooms were ostentatiously oversized considering the little use they would get, and contained all the modern technological gadgets that you could think of. It was like a collector's paradise, whether you were into the very old or the latest in technology.

The only thing the house lacked; and I felt that this was the most important part, was a soul. The building was as polished and cold as Liam.

The only pictures that lined the walls were Rembrandts or Van Goghs. Not a single personal photograph littered any of the surfaces of the antique sideboards, or tables. I thought it was all rather sad. Photographs were memories, times to remember with fondness. It also said a lot about Liam, and our relationship that there were none.

I walked through the front door, car keys in my right hand, towards the silver Aston Martin. It was a lovely car, but to me, it represented yet another item that Liam added to his collection.

I smiled to myself; at least this collector's item was getting out.

I slid into the leather seat and fired up the engine; it roared to life. The tyres ate at the miles like a kid eating its way through a box of candy.

Liam might think that he owned me, but I had learnt a thing of two from him.

Liam threw money at me, so that I always looked my best; in the last twelve months, I had taken advantage of this and smuggled quite a nice stash of cash into a bank account under my new name. Jessica Ripley was a girl of means. I had wanted to ensure that I could take care of myself, and like it or not I needed money to do that. Jessica's account boasted a cool two million, not to be sniffed at, and would do me more than nicely so that I could live out my life in comfort. I had even bought myself a small dwelling on the Isle of Skye in Scotland, which is where Charles and I were going to live out our lives together.

I couldn't stop the smile that spread across my lips at the thought of my new home. Proportionally it was small, but it was cosy and warm, and more importantly it had a soul. Happiness filled the cottage, and I was determined that that was the way it was going to stay.

Today I was shopping for Jessica, because Jessica didn't wear designer labels. No, today I was going to reinvent myself. I laughed, riding the high that my new life was going to give me.

Turning up the radio I sang at full throttle to Def Leppard – Let's get rocked.

Chapter Five

Liam

I tapped my fingers on the file that Pete Townend had presented to me just before ten a.m. Pete sat in one of the black leather-bound chairs in my office. The large antique oak desk separated us by four-foot.

I had a passion for collecting the best. My office was no exception to that. It was situated in an elevated position overlooking the River Ouse, which flows through York City Centre, where boats loaded with tourists happily chugged across it. The midmorning sun shone through the window, bouncing off the white painted walls. To the back of the office sat a deep red leather sofa, protected from the sun was a Rembrandt, which stood out against the stark whiteness of the walls. An oak filing cabinet was the only piece of modern furniture in the room. I didn't particularly like it, but it was a necessity.

The oak desk that I sat behind sat comfortably in the office space. I don't believe in littering my desk with personal photographs, and so the only items that sat on the deep red leather-bound desk top, was my Apple laptop, and a Caran dAche Cealograph Zenith 45, 18 Carat Rose Gold

Massif Fountain Pen, which I rolled against the leather surface of the desk. The 22 diamonds on the body of the pen sparkled in the sun light. The sparseness of my office made some people uncomfortable.

Clutter can tell you a lot about a person, it was one of the reasons I didn't partake in it.

Pete was sweating and my silence was eating away at him. "Her name is Chrissie Sanders." I looked up from the file and locked my eyes on Pete; he sweated a bit more heavily and wiped at his brow.

To some, Pete might look intimidating with his broad-set shoulders and thick rib of muscle that laced its way round a six-foot-eight frame. A scar lined Pete's left cheek, and his crooked nose only added to the hardness in his deep set brown black eyes. Pete kept his hair military short, adding to the badass image.

Pete normally dressed like he was ready for a fight, in loose-fitting clothes. Today, he wore a drab black polyester suit that was about two sizes too small. The fabric stretched as it wrapped around the thick muscles of Pete's arms. The trousers pulled at the legs and thighs. Nervously, Pete looped a finger round the collar of his off-white shirt; the skinny grey tie had been loosened some time ago.

I looked back down at the file. Pete's tanned skin lost a bit more colour. I'd say one thing for Pete, he had done an excellent job *this* time. I even had Chrissie's routine and timelines laid out before me. Fear can do that to a person, for some they needed that kind of motivation. I was more than happy to oblige.

"Well Pete, you have excelled yourself, this time." Pete relaxed at my words, such a silly boy. "Now there is a matter of your debt."

Pete sputtered. "What debt, I've provided the information you asked for, at no cost."

"Six years too late Pete, I should have had this to begin with." Pete sweated a bit more, and so he should. "If I added up the interest on the payment I made, well you can understand when I say I'm out of pocket. You took my money Pete, and didn't do the job you were paid to do, that's an awful lot of interest, especially at my rates, and now you're going to pay it back."

"What do you want?" I liked a man who knew when he was beat.

"I want her." I held up the photo of Chrissie. "And you're going to ensure I get her."

Pete paled.

Sweat trickled down his face like tears. I'd have to get the leather chair cleaned once he'd gone.

"I don't understand Mr Thornton, I can't just kidnap her." He could, but that wasn't what I wanted him to do, so I left the comment unsaid.

"Who said anything about kidnapping? Your problem, Pete, is you have no finesse. You're like a bulldozer." Pete's brow wrinkled. "You, Pete, are going to push her down the stairs at that multi-storey car park at the Coppergate Centre that she leaves her car in every Wednesday, making sure she hits her head hard."

"I'm sorry, I don't understand."

"Then I suggest you stop talking and let me finish," I snapped. I hated being interrupted. "Amnesia, Pete that is what I am talking about."

"But what happens if it doesn't work."

"The way I see it Pete, *you* have a fifty-fifty chance of it working. Let's just hope for you that the coin lands in your favour. If it doesn't, you won't need to worry abut next months rent."

I'd done a lot of research into amnesia. Unlike Pete, I'd looked at all the possibilities. The greater the trauma the greater the percentage of the brain closing off certain memories; add onto that a good whack to the head and the odds were stacked more in my favour. The brain was a clever thing in the way that it shut out memories that it felt it couldn't be dealt with. I recalled how my PA had been involved in a car accident; to this day Anne Clark could not remember anything leading up to or during the accident, her only memory was waking up in hospital.

Any memories Chrissie maintained could be explained away by displacement. I had worked it all out, it was going to work; it *had* to work. Oh, I have no doubt there would be someone in the medical profession that would disagree with my understanding of amnesia. But I was desperate, and I did not like the fact that I felt desperate about this. Once I'd seen Chrissie, I had found my solution to Kate's death, and I was not prepared to lose twice.

I looked over at Pete. "It is important that this appears as a mugging gone wrong. Today is Saturday so you have a few days to get yourself together. I will be there, because I am the one that will be reporting the mugging." What I really meant, and Pete knew this, was that I was going to be there to make sure that he didn't back out.

"I wish I'd never met you." Ah, a condemned man.

"Well you did. Like it or not Pete, I own you." I watched as Pete pushed himself out of the chair. His shoulders were slumped and his eyes never left the beige carpeted floor.

"Don't let me down Pete, not in this." I didn't need to say more, Pete knew when he was beat.

The door closed quietly behind Pete's retreating form.

I opened my laptop and studied my calendar. There was only one event that required both mine and Kate's attendance. It was Janine Walters' charity shindig over at Merchant Adventures. I didn't like the woman, middle class trying to be something that she could never be, so Kate's looming accident wouldn't be a problem when I sent my apologies.

I closed the file and smiled; for the first time since the bitch had told me she had cancer, I had a solution. I wasn't beaten and that mattered to me. I would not be beaten not like this, not by her, and her stupid cancer.

It never occurred to me that Chrissie would not have the same temperament as Kate, and despite them being identical twins, they were two separate people in their own right. I had controlled and manipulated a lot of people in my time. Chrissie was not going to be an exception to this.

Chapter Six

Kate

"If there are any changes, and you start to remember anything, please contact us." I looked at the policemen as they walked out the door of my hospital room.

I was more than a tad frustrated. I'd spent the last hour saying '*I can't remember*', to all the questions that one of the policemen had asked me; his buddy had looked a little less than impressed. I'm not quite sure if he'd thought that his brooding looks would kick start my memory, and everything would suddenly come rushing back to me. Well, it hadn't. And if he wasn't happy with my answers, then he ought to be *me*. Frustration was becoming a very familiar friend of mine.

I looked down at the photo album that lay at the end of the bed. I felt like kicking it. Its white leather-bound exterior seemed a stark reminder of everything I no longer was. I didn't open the book, what would be the point, I could relay every wedding photo there was of me and Liam, looking happy on our wedding day. I'd looked at each page at least fifty times now, hoping that my memory would come back to me. Frankly, being an outsider on your own wedding was not a good feeling.

I could no longer deny that Liam and I were married; he had brought me proof of that, and it was sat at the end of my bed, in all its white glory, laughing at me. I felt like running, running from everything, and everyone.

Liam's sister, Jenny, sat in the chair near my bed watching me, her hand lovingly placed on her round and very pregnant belly. A stab of pain, mixed with longing ran through me, twisting at my gut. For the hundredth time since Jenny had introduced herself to me I wondered why it hurt so much to see her pregnant form.

Did I want children?

I ran the question round my head, and didn't think that that was it. It was more of a need to see *my* child, and yet I knew from both Liam and Jenny that there were no children. It was a very odd and frightening feeling, to need something so badly, and yet to not understand why. To know that it never existed. There was no logic to apply to this feeling of mine.

Jenny smiled at me, and the smile reached her pale blue eyes. She was Liam's opposite. In fact, it was hard to believe that they were siblings. Where Liam was cold and remote, Jenny was full of warmth. Her cheeks were slightly flushed and I could tell she was tired.

"Why don't you go?" I asked for the tenth time.

Jenny shook her head sending her jaw length light brown hair to swing around her face. While Liam was on the thinner side, Jenny was well rounded in a healthy way. Her bone structure was thicker than Liam's. She was also a good deal taller, at over six foot. Given my lack of height she was like an Amazonian woman to me. Jenny wore a cotton summer yellow flowered dress. The pleats at the front made allowance for her bump. The soft yellow pumps complemented her dress.

"No, Liam wanted me to wait here while he called at the house to get you some fresh clothes." Liam, always bloody Liam, and what he *wanted*.

"Look Jenny, it's not like I'm going to leave here before he comes. As nice as my silk nightie is, people are going to notice. Go home." Jenny smiled but remained where she was.

"OK, have it your own way." I flopped against my pillows.

The doctor was letting me go home. Honestly, I wasn't so sure I wanted to go *home*. Maybe it was because I would then be alone with Liam. He still didn't do anything for me, and I certainly had no intention of having sex with him. I wondered how many headaches I could have, how many times I'd be able to say *'it's too soon'*, before he ran out of patience. I'd know soon enough, I guess.

"So how you feeling, other than tired?"

Jenny smiled at me, and leant back in her chair. "Scared."

I laughed. "It's the second time round you need to worry about, now that's scary, because you know what to expect."

"There isn't going to be a second time. I think this is going to be it."

"You don't mean that. What happened to the girl that said ten minutes ago she wanted at least six?"

Jenny giggled, it was a nice sound. "I've changed my mind."

"You can't do that; ten minutes is too soon for changing your mind. You have to leave it until at least a year or so, or until you start feeling broody again."

"Yeah, well, that's a pregnant lady for you."

I looked up at the ceiling. "You know it's strange, because I can tell you how it feels to be pregnant. How uncomfortable you can get the further along in the pregnancy

49

you get. How it feels to want to sleep on my side, but being unable to do so because of my bump. I can tell you about the immense love you're going to feel for that little person inside you. And yet I've never had kids, so why do I have these feelings?" A tear fell from the corners of my eyes.

Jenny reached across and took my hand. "I wish I had some answers for you, Kate, I really do." I could hear the sadness in her voice and felt like a bitch for being this way.

"It doesn't matter. I'm going to be an aunt. I get to spoil my niece, fill her full of sugar and hand her back to her mum and dad."

"Don't you dare, and no drum kits either."

"I wasn't thinking of a drum kit, after all she will have to have some finesse if Uncle Liam is going to spend *any* kind of time with her. So, I was thinking of starting her off with a recorder, and then getting a violin when the kid turns four."

"I think I'd rather have a drum kit."

"Well, I'm betting Uncle Liam wouldn't." I turned my head and looked at Jenny, smiling.

"You're probably right, though I don't think he would be that crazy on any musical instrument."

We laughed at each other, as the door to my room opened. Liam stood in the doorway, a frown on his face. I looked at his expensive soft pinstripe black suit and began to wonder if he ever wore anything else. In his left hand was a small leather bound overnight bag. I didn't bother to read which designer signature was on it.

"The doctor says you can leave whenever you're ready." Liam placed the bag on the bed, his sharp blue eyes taking in the scene before him.

I'd bet he didn't miss much.

I took the bag and looked inside. Pulling out a pair of cream Chanel wide-leg linen trousers and a pale pink silk shirt with three quarter sleeves, I eyed them with suspicion.

"Are we going somewhere?"

Liam blinked. "No."

I pulled out the three-inch strappy pink sandals and began to wonder if Liam was for real. "Do I normally get this dressed up to sit in a car? I'm only going home, so why do I have to get decked out?"

Jenny placed a hand on my arm.

I ignored it.

"Three-inch heels Liam, *really?*" From the way his cheeks had reddened I would say he was getting annoyed at me.

"Just go in the bathroom and get changed, Kate." I guess we weren't going to discuss this.

I sighed, given that this was the only clothing I had, there really wasn't much choice. I took the clothes, shoes and bag into the bathroom. Closing the door, I leaned back on it, dropping the clothing on the floor. Of all the stupid things to bring; I wanted to be comfy, not dripping in designer wear for Liam. In fact, I didn't want to get dressed in anything that Liam liked.

Opening the door twenty minutes later I stood in the clothes, with the killer sandals tied securely to my feet. The sandals were made to look nice. They were not made with feet in mind. They were nipping at my toes, and eating into my ankles where the strap tied.

"You haven't put any makeup on." I raised my eyes to the ceiling.

"I'm going home, Liam, to sit down in the garden and relax. We do have a garden, don't we?"

"Of course, we have a garden. Now I would appreciate it if you would put some makeup on."

I looked at Liam and narrowed my eyes. "Well it's my face and I don't want to." I'd have taken a step forward and stomped to the bed, but I knew I wouldn't be able to do it with any grace in these sandals.

Liam's cheeks reddened and a sharp stab of anger entered his blue eyes as he looked at me. His fist clenched and unclenched at his sides. "Put the makeup on Kate." Liam's voice was even, despite his obvious anger.

"Here Kate, let me help you." Jenny rose from the chair and waddled over to me, a hand resting on her large belly.

I wanted to tell her to take a hike. I sighed instead and walked back into the bathroom, while Liam walked over to the window, ignoring me. Jenny closed the bathroom door behind her.

"What's wrong Kate, this is so unlike you." Jenny looked worried, and I wondered if she was worried about me, or Liam.

"A blow to the head can do that to a person." Jenny cringed and I felt guilty. "Sorry, I guess I'm being a grouch."

"It's OK, you're allowed to be."

"No, I shouldn't take it out on you." I stared at the makeup I didn't want to wear. It was now more out of principle than anything else.

Jenny smiled at me opening the makeup bag. "Why is Liam so insistent on the makeup? Look at me; I look dressed for a dinner date, not to go home and convalesce."

"You know Liam, he is all about appearances." No, I didn't know Liam. Jenny gave me a long look. "You don't normally disagree with him."

"You mean I'm a pushover."

"No, I'd say, normally, you're more compliant."

"I still sound like a pushover."

Jenny smiled. "Come let's get this done."

52

I eyed the makeup bag and with a sigh took it from Jenny's outstretched hand. Ten minutes later we both walked out of the bathroom. Liam turned and smiled when he saw the light coating of makeup. I felt as though I had lost something very significant, a fight I shouldn't have lost, as I saw the look of satisfaction that crossed Liam's face.

I hobbled to the bed, coming to a stop a metre away from where Liam stood. "Well, can we go now?" I flipped my hair back.

"Yes," Liam was a man of few words, especially when he'd just got his own way.

"I'll come and see you later Kate." Jenny leaned forward and kissed my cheek, before she walked out the room.

I had the overwhelming desire to grab her arm, and beg her not to leave me alone with Liam. Instead, my heart flipping in my chest, I watched her leave, saying nothing.

Liam bent and picked up the white leather overnight bag; taking the makeup bag and crumpled silk nightie out of my hands, he put them in the overnight bag. Placing a hand on my back he led me out the room. Fear struck me; I was going to a house I couldn't remember, to live with a man I didn't know, or like. The hospital suddenly felt like my best option, and I didn't want to leave. The pressure of Liam's hand on my back got my feet moving. In a daze of unease, I walked down the corridor of the hospital. It buzzed with life and low chatter.

As we left the hospital Liam pulled out the car keys from his trouser pocket. I stared ahead as he continued to steer me. We stopped at the boot of a black Bentley. I wasn't into cars, but I knew a Bentley when I saw its badge. Liam dropped the bag in the boot; the boot lid snapped shut with a dull thump. My heart gave a jump. I had to get a grip of this fear; otherwise, I was going to be a nervous wreck. I walked away from Liam's guiding hand and opened the front passenger door. The smell of rich leather accosted my senses as I slid inside. The cars plush interior did nothing for me; it was what I was starting to think of as '*typical Liam*'. Only the best was good enough. I should be flattered that Liam had chosen me to be his wife, the best of all the women he had met. Well, I wasn't impressed at all.

I looked out the window as we set off for *home*. Liam thankfully wasn't a big talker so there was no small talk.

The scenery passed by merging into one, and before I knew it I was staring at a large white monstrous building. The house spread before me like an ivory palace. I stumbled as I walked across the block paving towards it.

I suddenly felt tired.

Tired of being afraid, of not knowing anything about my past. All I had, were feelings that came and went. And the little voice in my head that said none of this was real, that I was experiencing this for the very first time. It was my first time to this house, my first time sitting in Liam's Bentley.

I guess that was amnesia for you.

Liam stood next to me and slowly we made our way into the house. The front door swung open and I caught my first glimpse of the inside.

The first thing that struck me was that it was very impersonal, cold even.

The staircase swept before me, threading left to right and meeting in the middle. White marble lay under my feet making up the large entrance hall, and continued up the elaborate staircase; cold and uninviting. A large chandelier poured down from the high ceiling in small droplets. To my right was a painting, it looked old and expensive. I walked forward, looking around for any hint of my past life.

"Why are there no photographs?" I turned to look at Liam.

"We have paintings." Not really an answer, but I could tell it was the only one I was going to get.

"Come, I'll take you to your room, so you can freshen up." My eyebrows rose into my hairline. Why on earth would I need to freshen up? Liam's hand pressed itself against my back and steered me up the staircase. We came to a stop in front of a white door.

My heart beat sped up; I wasn't so sure if it had to do with what lay behind the door, or the fact that Liam was taking me up to the bedroom. Not that I expected him to jump me as we entered, however the significance of it was not lost on me. I really didn't want to be here with Liam.

The door opened and I expelled a breath; the room was massive. A large wooden bed sat against the rear wall. I reckon I could lie in that bed and do a starfish, and not touch Liam. Again, there were no photographs, or come to that even paintings. The dressing table opposite the bed contained a mass of pots containing creams and makeup.

Liam dropped the white bag on the bed. He sent me a look that I couldn't fathom. "This is your room, mine is in the north wing."

Surprise hit me. "Why do we have separate rooms? Is there something wrong with us?" I should have felt relieved, but I didn't.

"There is nothing wrong with our relationship Kate, it is what it is." With that Liam closed the door and I was left alone.

The only thing left for me to do was go exploring, for something more comfortable to wear. Maybe I had some jogging pants somewhere. I looked around the room. No wardrobe. Hmm, guess I should start opening doors. The first door I opened was to the bathroom. It was smaller than the bedroom, but only just. The second door led to a large walk-in wardrobe / dressing room. Racks and racks of designer clothes hung along the walls, shoes and handbags sat on the shelving beneath. A long-padded bench ran down the middle of the room. I'd probably need a sit down while I decided what to *'freshen up'* into.

I took the killer sandals off; my feet pulsed in relief. Feet now happy I began to look through the contents of the clothes. After twenty minutes, I came to the conclusion that I never relaxed. There were no jogging pants or jeans. There were, however, running clothes and trainers, and I considered changing into one of the running outfits, but Liam's outraged face flitted before my eyes, and I thought better of it. Instead, I selected a lightweight cotton dress. It was a bit posh for sitting around in, but as there didn't seem to be anything else that said *comfort* to me, I decided that it would do.

Minutes later I stood before the floor to ceiling mirror in the dressing room, and thought I didn't look half bad. The cut and bruise on my head was starting to recede, and if I positioned my hair at an angle it hid a bit of it. I swung round and the soft yellow fabric of the dress swished round my thighs. Pulling at the little cap sleeves and running my hands down the length of the dress, I felt more like me, for the first time. Comfy even. I picked up the clothes I'd taken off and hung them up. I'd only worn them for a few hours, so they didn't need washing.

Barefoot I walked out of the dressing room and into the bathroom. Removing the makeup, I'd applied I smiled at my reflection.

Liam be damned.

Chapter Seven

Jessica

The smell of fresh brewing coffee woke me. I raised my hands above my head and stretched out; a soft smile played on my lips at the sound of footsteps, and the tinkering of cups clicking together.

I felt so relaxed, happy even.

I couldn't remember a time that I had ever felt so happy and content.

It had been four weeks since Kate Thornton had died. Liam had never tried to contact me during the few days I had stayed at the centre, before I'd moved on to start my new life. I had left no forwarding address at the centre, and while the staff seemed to be concerned they had let me go. Given that I had come in refusing to take any type of medication, I think that they had been relieved to see me go. They were not there after all to watch me die, but to help me live a more comfortable existence, if that were possible. Charles had helped to pacify even the most persistent of nurses, doctors and carers. At first I had been nervous, worried, and scared to hell that Liam would come to the centre. That no matter where I went he would find me, because he knew about

Jessica Ripley. About Charles and I, but as the days ticked by and turned to weeks, I'd stopped looking over my shoulder and started to live the life I had wanted so badly.

I watched Charles as he came into view. My eyes travelled the length of his body, and there was a lot to take in. Charles was completely naked. His body was made to be admired, and I was happy to take in every glorious muscled inch of his tanned skin. From his long well sculptured legs and round pert bum. A six pack that would make any girl want to run her fingers along, just to feel the corded muscle beneath. His thick black hair fell forward briefly hiding his hazel eyes. My smile widened. The things I intended to do to that body, made my smile widen even more, if that were possible. Had I been a cat I would be purring in anticipation.

"Good morning, Gorgeous." His voice was husky.

"You know, I don't think I could ever get used to this. I don't think I want get used to it, I like this happy contented feeling too much to take it for granted." I pushed the pillows against the headboard and sat up letting the bed sheet drop to my waist, revealing my breasts. Charles eyes darkened with desire and I laughed.

"Tease." Charles passed me a cup of steaming coffee.

"Oh, I'm not a tease, because once I've drunk this I fully intend to back it up." Charles threw his head back and laughed. I shivered at the sound, tingles of anticipation running down my spine.

"Come here." Charles grabbed me and I nestled into his body, sipping at my coffee, and absently circling a finger along his abs.

"Happy?" I asked, because it was important to me that Charles felt as happy as I did.

"Happy can't cover everything I'm feeling."

"So, no regrets, you gave up a lot to come here with me." Here was a three-bedroomed whitewashed old

58

farmhouse/cottage in Portree on the Isle of Skye. The farmhouse sat in 38 acres of beautiful unspoilt grass land. On a clear day, you could see the sea as it lapped at the shoreline in the distance. The rooms in the farmhouse were cosy, not small, but not supersized either. I loved each one of them, from the large inglenook fireplace stacked high with logs, ready to be thrown onto the log burner, to the country kitchen with its oak cupboards, and Aga, gently working away to heat the house and provide hot water.

The remoteness of the house was what I loved the most. I never got tired of watching the birds swoop and dive; of hearing them singing to each other. The hedgehog that liked to walk up to the front door, and sniff round the potted plants for slugs; which I had nicknamed Spike. It all made me feel at home, that I belonged here.

"No regrets. The practice here is smaller, but the people are fantastic. I hadn't realised how impersonal everything had become until I started working at the clinic here."

I snuggled closer into Charles. "I love it here, and I love you." I reached across Charles and put my now empty coffee cup down on the bedside table. Taking Charles' cup from him I placed it next to mine. Hands free, I cupped Charles' face between my hands. "Thank you," I whispered, then I kissed him long, slowly and thoroughly.

An hour later we stood looking in the garden where a forgotten vegetable patch had once resided, and, of which had been invaded by weeds. A gentle breeze caressed my skin and played with my hair, which I had tied back loosely into a low ponytail. We were lucky that we were having such a lovely summer. Scotland, after all, was not renowned for dry sunny weather.

The farmhouse was unprotected, from the harsh weather that raked this beautiful land, and we had spent the first week or so, ensuring that the walls were sealed with a new lick of paint, and that and the roof was weather tight. It had been hard work. We had both flopped down on an evening after our hard labour exhausted but happy.

"So, what are you wanting to grow?"

I looked at the patch of weeds. "I was thinking of potatoes, cabbage, carrots, onions and cauliflowers. Oh, and maybe some beetroot. I also fancy establishing a herb garden to the right near the window. I thought if we put them into big pots it might help to discourage the slugs."

Charles gave the patch of land in front of us a considering look. "I'm not so sure you're going to fit all that in. You'll need to give them room to grow."

I smiled at Charles. "Since we have to dig out all the weeds, I thought we could extend the patch."

"Are you trying to keep me busy, so I won't go looking for trouble?"

"Oh, Baby, I'm the only trouble you're ever going to need." I leaned into Charles and gave his left bum cheek a squeeze.

He laughed and grabbed me. "You know, if you keep this up, we're never going to get anything done."

"You're right, you're just going to have to learn to control yourself."

"*Me!*" I laughed at the astonished look on his face.

"I'm not sure I know what you're implying here." I tried very hard to look serious.

"You're not, huh." With that, Charles grabbed me and lifted me into his arms. "Then I guess I'm just going to have to show you."

"What in the vegetable patch?" I squealed.

"It'll give you something to smile about, while you plant all those vegetables.

He was right about that.

Chapter Eight

Kate

I stood in my bedroom looking at the dress that Liam had laid on my bed. There really wasn't much to it. The washing label was bigger than the fabric used to make the thing.

The Armani label said it cost a fortune, and it was nothing but a scrap of fabric.

The more I looked at the dress the angrier I became. It was a lovely dress, even if there wasn't much of it. The designer had gone to a lot of trouble to make the dress look classy rather than trashy, so I guess I should be grateful about that. No, it wasn't the dress, it was the fact that Liam, had come into *my* bedroom, and had chosen what *I* was to wear, like I had no taste. How could I possibly have got it wrong with a room full of designer wear, was, what I would have liked to know. I don't think that my lack of memory could have also affected my capability of what was appropriate attire.

The only good thing about Liam stomping in here, was that it had been the only time he had. In fact, since my return, other than a peck on the cheek, or a guiding hand on my back, Liam had not made any effort to touch me.

This pleased me, and also worried me.

I may have lost my memory, but it didn't mean that I didn't know something was wrong. Maybe he was waiting for me to start to remember things. I don't know. It just sort of worried me, because I didn't like the fact that I felt totally beholden to him. This was his house; the clothes in the dressing room were what Liam had bought me. In fact, other than what Liam provided me with, I didn't have anything.

No friends had come around to see me.

There were no worried parents. Just me, here, to be owned by Liam.

I felt like a piece of furniture to Liam, dressed up to look pretty, with bouts of usefulness.

It was now seven, and I was aware that I wasn't dressed, and that apart from showering I had done little to get ready. This was the tenth charity function we had been to since I arrived, and I was getting to the point that all I wanted to do was slob in front of the telly and watch a rerun of Friends. They all seemed to be having a lot more fun than I was. What people failed to realise is that these charity functions weren't about raising money, as much as it was a way for people to show off their wealth. Connections were made, deals arranged, appointments made. All the while people smiled and pretended to feel something for the charity on the agenda that night.

Liam walked back into my room, dressed in a black tux. "What's going on, you're not ready." I could see his patience slipping away.

"I don't think I feel up to going tonight, why don't you go on your own, just this once." I tried to ensure that my voice held all the tiredness that I felt.

"You're going."

My eyes widened in irritation. "And I said I don't want to."

"Kate, don't push me on this."

I sighed. "Liam, I'm not trying to push you anywhere, I simply want to sit this one out. I'm exhausted."

"Put the dress on and get your hair and makeup fixed. I'll be back in ten minutes. By then I want you in that dress and ready to leave."

"I'm not going to put the dress on." I folded my arms across my chest, tilting my head to a stubborn angle.

Before I knew what was happening, Liam's fist shot forward and punched me in the chest. The force of it, plus the fact that I wasn't prepared, sent me skittering backwards into the bedpost; my right arm took the brunt of the fall before I went crashing to the floor.

"Why are you being like this? Why can't you just be Kate?" Liam looked down at me, distain clear on his face.

My dressing gown had become untied and was draped across my body showing a large red patch on my arm, where I'd hit the bedpost, the skin was quickly darkening and a bruise was forming. My breathing was coming in gasps as I tried to breeze through the pain in my chest from Liam's blow, and rework how to breathe around the tightness that had formed there. A bruise the perfect size of Liam's fist had already started to come out on my chest.

Liam sighed, but made no move to come closer. "You can't wear that dress now, look at you." I sat where I was, not speaking or moving.

Liam marched into the dressing room, coming back moments later with a long sleeved sparkly gold dress that touched the floor. The front was cut high and the back low. "This will have to do. You have ten minutes." He threw the dress on the bed and slammed the bedroom door.

Hands shaking, I pushed myself up. My legs were like jelly, and it was though all bone had been removed; with nothing to give them substance they gave way.

Luckily, I fell onto the bed, rather than the floor. I couldn't remember ever feeling this way before. My mind was in shock. Since the feeling was new to me, I concluded that this must have been the first time that Liam had ever hit me, or that I had ever been hit in such a way.

One thing was clear, I had to get out, of here.

Once the line of violence had been crossed, there was nothing stopping Liam doing it again. The second time was always easier until it just became a pattern. A pattern I wasn't sticking around to see come into fruition.

Right now, though, time was ticking, and I had to get that dress on, and my hair and makeup done. I wasn't beat, not just yet, I told myself. I was doing what I had to do. I pushed myself off the bed and picked up the dress. My hands still shook a little and my legs felt like I was walking through treacle, but I'd be ready, no matter what.

Liam came into the room exactly ten minutes later. I was ready. Hair piled up on top if my head in a tight thick bun. My makeup was light, and apart from my wedding ring and engagement ring I wore no jewellery, allowing the dress to do the talking.

Liam nodded his head in satisfaction; holding the door open he inclined his head, indicating that I needed to start moving. The gold sparkly shoes were a continuation of the dress, and though stunning to look at, they were not comfy, nor were they made for walking in. Six inch spiked heels dug into the carpet, the pile preventing the heels from slipping. I was dreading the walk down the marble landing and staircase. With a deep breath, I walked past Liam and onto the marble. Carefully I made my way across the cold marble. Funny we had so much of the stuff. It resonated with Liam's personality, pitch perfect against my heels.

We arrived at Henry Henderson's house, the host of tonight's charity bash, a fashionable fifteen minutes late. I didn't get the politics concerning what time was considered fashionably late, and what constituted bad manners. If someone turned up at the dentist fifteen minutes late, they wouldn't smile and shake your hand. You'd have lost your appointment, and paid for the privilege of missing it as well.

An orchestra was situated in the curve of the sweeping staircase, their music echoing around the room. Acoustically the vastness of the room allowed for the music to travel upward, and bounce off the walls and high ceiling. It echoed back to me, sweeping me away to a feeling of nostalgia, where I laid upon the cold tiles of a kitchen floor, a glass of champagne dangling from my right hand, as I threw back my head and laughed. A feeling of complete happiness bubbled around me, and I couldn't believe that it was actually me feeling this way. I felt loved, completely and utterly loved. Warm masculine arms snaked around my waist pulling me down. I sloshed champagne everywhere as I allowed those arms to pull at me.

"Kate." Liam spoke in my ear, a harsh whisper that brought me back to the present with an unpleasant snap. I looked at Liam; those arms had not been his.

I blinked away the remaining memory, sad to see it go, wondering if it would ever return. A coldness brushed against my skin, replacing the warmth of the long-forgotten memory. It was the first real memory I had had. I plastered a smile on my lips and allowed Liam to lead me further into the room. We were eagerly met by hungry wannabes, all wanting Liam's attention. They turned to me, spreading on the charm as they took my hand and gave it a gentle shake, commenting on how beautiful I looked. Liam soaked it up, as if the compliments were for him. In a way, I guess they were.

I grabbed a glass of champagne as the waiter walked past, his silver tray littered with the stuff. In the far corner, I saw Jenny. Making my excuses, I made my way to her. She was dressed in a pale blue chiffon dress that accentuated her bump. A bump she made no effort to hide. Jenny was already one very proud mum to be.

"Hey, what are you doing hiding away in the corner?" A smile played across my lips.

"Oh, I'm not hiding, just people watching. They're like vultures, aren't they?" I looked back to where Liam stood holding court, his sharp blue eyes assessing everyone and everything, missing nothing.

"Hmm, though if I were a vulture I don't I think I'd be best pleased to have them called one; I'd consider it a slight on my kind." Jenny sent me a sharp glance.

"So, you got your bag all packed and ready?" I asked, grabbing her attention. Her frown disappeared and a smile spread across her face.

"I've had it packed, unpacked and repacked at least a hundred times. Denis is finding the whole thing rather funny."

"Ah, teachers, they have a strange concept on life, and the funny side of it." Jenny's husband was a professor at York University.

"Now, you're being mean." She tapped me lightly on the left arm with her wine glass full of orange juice.

I laughed at her. The reference I'd made to Denis being a teacher rather than a professor had made her eyebrows draw into her hairline. "I just enjoy winding you two up. It's hard to say which one of you will bite first."

Jenny smiled at me and took a sip of orange juice. "So how is everything going with you and Liam? Do you remember anything yet?"

I looked at Jenny. She knew some of her brother's faults, the controlling issues he had about his life, and everything in it. I don't think she knew, or would guess that he would physically abuse his wife. "Why do you suppose he's so controlling? I've always liked surprises myself." Jenny gave me a sharp look; either she caught the undercurrent of bitterness in my voice or she was very perceptive. "Liam and I seem to live separate lives. I never really see him, apart from when he needs to dress me up and show me off."

Jenny placed a light hand on my right arm. I tried not to wince, because even the lightest of touches seemed to hurt. "He's always been that way. In time, hopefully when you start to remember things, it won't seem so bad." Jenny loved her brother; I wished I had someone that loved me as much.

My mind flicked back to the memory of feeling so completely loved and happy, as I lay on the cold kitchen floor. I couldn't tell Jenny about it, how could I? Liam was her brother, and the memory and feeling felt so strong that I knew without doubt that I loved, and still loved whoever those arms belonged to.

"Why don't I have any friends?" I tried to look relaxed as I asked the question. "No one has come over to see me, well apart from you. Denis doesn't count, he's a tagalong. Doesn't it seem rather odd to you?" I looked at Liam as he began to circulate, I'd have to join him soon; he'd already looked over at me a couple of times arching a brow at me.

"You have me, I'm a friend, and I come and see you." Jenny looked slightly worried.

"I didn't mean to discount you as a friend Jenny, it's just I never see anyone else. Where are my parents?"

"Liam hasn't told you anything?" Her eyebrows lifted into her hairline.

"Nope, not a thing. As I said, we don't really seem to see much of each."

"Your parents died when you were a baby, I think you were adopted and then when they died you went to live with an aunt, who, well, wasn't much of a parent figure."

I really hadn't had a lot of luck in life, if it could be summed up so briefly. "Go on, tell me more about this aunt.

Is she living somewhere close? Seeing her might help kick start my memories."

"I don't think seeing her would be a good idea."

"Why do you say that? Come on, give me something here, stop being so vague." I sent Jenny a pointed look.

"Your aunt is in prison." I'd pushed.

"What did she do?"

"Drugs." There wasn't much more to say. "When Liam met you, she was trying to sell you on, you have a certain appeal Kate, and not just to men, I've seen one or two ladies looking at you, with a little more interest than what would be considered appropriate. Liam finds it funny." I watched Jenny; her eyes followed Liam around the room. "Liam liked the idea of rescuing you from a life not worth living. But I think that it's your extraordinary beauty that made him take you in and marry you. The only thing that Liam asked of you is that you sever all links and ties with your old life. I think he was worried keeping them in your life would drag you down."

I looked at Jenny. Well, I had wanted to know. "Thanks, I think."

"Sorry."

"No, I had wanted to know. Well I'd best go and join Liam, I have a feeling I have loitered here too long."

Jenny smiled. "How do you fancy meeting for lunch tomorrow? I still have a few things I need to get, before this little one is born. I've only got a couple of months to go and with it being my first I don't want to leave things until last minute."

"I would ask what you could possibly need. I've seen the nursery and the rest. That baby already has more than it needs. Lunch though, now that sounds good. However, I have not failed to notice that with Denis lecturing, I reckon you're looking for another packhorse to carry your bags."

Jenny laughed, "When did you become such a pessimist Kate?"

"Since I've seen you shop." I gave her a hug and made my way to Liam. His ears had started to turn red, he was getting mad.

I had a feeling that that anger was directed at me.

"I'll ring you tomorrow morning, to firm everything up." I waved at Jenny to let her know I'd heard her.

Chapter Nine

Liam

I watched Kate as she talked with Jenny. There was an air of confidence about her that my Kate had never had. It had a certain appeal. I'd noticed more than a few people give Kate a second glance. The dress that she wore accentuated her slim figure. It moulded to her body, hugging at her waist and caressing her breasts. The front of the dress was cut high falling gracefully across her collar bone, while the back dipped past her waist. The soft caramel of her skin blended perfectly with the shimmering gold of her dress.

Her left leg was on full few, the deep slit in the dress stopped at her thigh. The beautiful cut of muscle along her high thigh highlighted her love of running. The dress suited her confidence, in a way that it had never suited the real Kate. While I cared for the dress, and appreciated the vision of beauty that was the new Kate, I didn't care for the confidence that radiated from her.

My Kate had always had an air of vulnerability that had appealed to me more. It was that weakness that had made Kate pliable, she certainly wouldn't have argued with me, the way this new Kate had.

I'd noticed the wince that lined her face as Jenny lightly touched her arm. I hadn't meant to hit her, it had just happened. I had come to the conclusion in those brief seconds it had taken for my fist to contact her chest that I needed to get rid of Chrissie.

Chrissie was the problem; if I had to beat Chrissie out of Kate, I would.

I'd do whatever I needed to.

I had to admit to myself that it had never occurred to me, that Chrissie wouldn't be as submissive as Kate, they were identical twins after all, a carbon copy of the other. Chrissie was Kate now, and she needed to learn how to behave.

I'd seen a few roving eyes stray Kate's way as she'd laughed with Jenny. The tinkling of her laughter rose above the noise of the orchestra, like the tinkling of soft bells. Enticing and enchanting.

Those two were getting on better than ever. It was just as well that I had been careful what I had told Jenny. Jenny knew about the aunt, and drugs. She did not know about the sister. At the time, it seemed irrelevant. Now, well, it was a secret best kept hidden.

I arched a brow at Kate as I caught her eye. The laughter instantly left her eyes. I suppose I should feel guilty. I didn't. Guilt was something that I had long given up feeling, that and forgiveness. She would learn to keep herself in line. If she resisted, well she deserved all that she got. I was not a violent man, however sometimes it just couldn't be helped.

"Kate is looking particularly lovely tonight." I turned to face the host of tonight's event.

Henry Henderson was made money; they were the worse. They had no finesse. They were loud and brash, throwing money around as though to prove their worth. Money should speak quietly. It was power, not an ornament to be dangled in front of everyone's noses. Before the year

71

was up I'd bankrupt Henry Henderson and put him back where he belonged.

Nevertheless, I smiled at Henry, until our deal was signed I could play nice. "Henry, you really have outdone yourself tonight."

Henry beamed. I threw another look in Kate's direction, which got her moving towards me. Stupid bitch, did she not realise she was here to mingle, not hide in a corner talking to Jenny.

"Kate, I was just saying how lovely you look tonight." Henry took Kate's delicate hand between the palms of his chubby hands. The man really didn't have many redeeming features. Sweat lined the young man's forehead. Henry needed to lose a few stone, and then some. Henry was in his late twenties, though with all the extra weight he totted around and slobby jowls, you would be forgiven for putting an extra ten, fifteen years on the man.

The tux Henry wore was made from good quality cloth. The cut had been designed to trim him at the waist. The only problem was that the tux was made for a man much slimmer, in fact a man three times thinner. The jacket couldn't be fastened, and the trousers stretched into creases of stress at his thighs.

Kate smiled at Henry, quickly slipping her hand from his. "Why Henry, you are too gracious."

Henry chuckled, ogling Kate. "The auction starts soon, I was wondering if Kate would care to help?"

I looked at Henry, could the man not organise anything, how crass to expect a guest to help sell the merchandise. "Where's Jane?" Jane was Henry's wife. She was as skinny as Henry was fat, with a loud mouth and terrible grating voice. I could understand why Henry would not want his wife being the centre of attention.

"She's putting little Jamie to bed." The world was not a blessed place. Jamie, was eight and was the reason for

72

tonight's charity event. The boy suffered from a heart problem. Henry had once gone into detail about it, but really why the hell did I care?

Like his mother the boy had no taste, and had a loud mouth. Jamie also had the misfortune to have Henry's taste for food. You would have thought that they would rally round the kid, and show him a healthy lifestyle. Not the Henderson's.

"It would be my pleasure." Henry beamed at Kate.

"Perfect, perfect." With a guiding hand, Henry led Kate to the front room, which had been cleared ready for the auction. Tonight's themed auction was fine wine. All the guests had been asked to donate, and now we got the chance to buy it back at an inflated price, while patting ourselves on the back, for helping raise money for yet another good cause.

Henry's voice sounded through the microphone, and like mindless sheep we all walked into the front room. The furniture had been moved aside replaced with chairs lined in a row. I loitered at the back, so that I could look at the crowd that had gathered. Kate stood on the temporary stage. There was a grace about Kate that I had always liked; Chrissie had the same grace. It commanded attention.

With a burst of activity, the auction began. Bottle after bottle was put up for auction. Tammy Sinclair jumped up from her seat, hand raised as she increased the bidding to a thousand pounds. Her large breasts bobbed about, threatening to break free of the skimpy red fabric that didn't quite contain them properly, but did at least give some cover. Tammy was our residence alcoholic. She would drink anything. Her husband, Jeremy, grabbed her arm and pulled her back down to her chair. Whispering harshly in her ear. Tammy jerked her arm out from his grasp, and slunk down in her chair, sulking like a toddler. Jeremy was always threatening to divorce her. It wouldn't do him any good, all the money was Tammy's, and he knew it. I couldn't understand why Jeremy didn't just lock Tammy away in a well-stocked wine cellar, and let nature take its course. Tammy's liver surely couldn't take much more?

Paula Clarkson sniggered into the ear of her latest husband. At sixty-seven, Paula was pumped full of enough Botox to stop any type of emotion from crossing her face. Paula's first husband, and the one whose money she was now spending, had died of a heart attack five years into their marriage. At thirty-two, Paula had been a stunning widow; she had spent the last thirty-five years taking up with any young man that was willing and able. Paula, however, had style, and the simple black dress was one of Chanel's finest. It fit her body perfectly. The plastic surgeons and health farms made sure that Paula had kept her thirty-two-year-old shape.

I saw Paula's eyes linger on Kate. Paula had always disliked Kate. Kate was a natural beauty, and Paula couldn't tolerate that. I smiled because I liked to see envy for what was mine. John Templeton, dashing and very young, in his early twenties, with blond hair and sky blue eyes, Paula's latest flame cum husband, was positively drooling as he watched Kate's body move smoothly around the stage, her left leg flashing from between the golden fabric of her dress. I felt something stir within me, something I hadn't felt in a long time. Desire for the woman that I had made mine. It was totally unexpected. And I renewed my interest in Kate. She felt my eyes on her and looked my way. The sparkle in her eyes died a little, and I felt irritation replace desire. It was probably as well.

With the last bottle sold, I walked forward to write a cheque for four thousand, and reclaim my bottle of champagne. Kate stood by my side. Henry's wife had finally made an appearance towards the end of the auction and had replaced Kate. I had heard a few groans from the audience when Jane had stepped up onto the stage, and Kate had stepped down.

Jane was dressed in a see-through emerald green floor length dress, which hugged her body. The dress didn't allow her to wear any type of underwear. Sequins clustered in groups covering certain parts of her anatomy. The colour should have been perfect for her, with her red hair. It wasn't. Of course, it didn't help that Jane's ample and vein laced tits were all but on show. Given her rake thin frame, the tits stood out like two manmade mountains within a flat plain.

"Thanks for looking after things while I put Jamie to bed. He has such terrible trouble getting off to sleep. I think it's from all the surgery he had when he was a baby." Jane's gratefulness was as shallow as the space between her tits.

Kate smiled. "It was a pleasure."

Tony Carlton stood behind Jane, with his dark brooding looks, chiselled features and strong jawline, his latest conquest hanging off his arm, a dreamy look on her face as she stared at him. I heard Tony cough and mutter that the pleasure had most definitely been the audience's; it was a shame that it had been taken away so swiftly. I noticed that Jane had heard Tony's drunken comments and her eyes narrowed on Kate. I pulled Kate into the crook of my arm, because I wouldn't put it past Jane to take a swing. The woman had no class and also had a reputation for taking a swing at people.

"Jane, it has been a lovely evening." I took Jane's hand and firmly held it in mine. Her attention swung to me and she smiled. Kate forgotten for now.

Our goodbyes said, we made our way to the limo in silence.

The silence continued all the way home.

Chapter Ten

Liam

I walked into the study, switching on the light, shadows cast against the darkly painted red walls. A small window sat along the wall in front of me. I didn't like too much natural light when I worked here, and I also needed to think about protecting the Rembrandt that hung on the back wall opposite my desk. The answer machine flashed from where it sat on the mahogany desk, in my study. I looked at it, irritation made tiny lines appear at the corner of my eyes. Kate's footsteps echoed on the stairs as she made her way to her room.

With a sigh, I sat down at the desk and pressed the button. Henry Henderson's voice boomed down the phone. "Liam, sorry to ring you so late." I'd just left his charity function so he knew I'd be up, so why start with an apology. I hated it when people felt the need to apologise. I never felt such a compulsion, so why did others. "Paula has just been saying that she saw Kate at a cancer clinic a month or so ago, and well, Jane and I, just wanted to ring and let you know that we are here for you and Kate." Jane's voice echoed in the background, bleating out words of comfort, that she didn't mean. "Of course, Paula could have got it wrong, she said she was in a state because her uncle had been taken in that very same day. She said that she wouldn't have thought much to it, but Kate was carrying a bag and, well, why would she need a bag if she was just visiting someone. Well, anyway, like I said, Jane and I are here for you. I just wanted to let you know. It's dreadful news, dreadful, Kate, poor Kate. Call me if you want to reschedule our appointment on Monday." Jane was still saying how sorry she was when the receiver hit the cradle.

I sat in the dim light looking at the answer machine, wanting to smash my fist into it. My hands shook with rage. How dare Henry Henderson pretend to try and understand how I was feeling?

I took a deep breath.

I had to focus.

I was not the type of person that panicked over such matters.

Apart from Charles, no one else knew about Kate's cancer. Paula, well I'd see to her, stop the gossip before it began. Instinct told me to arrange for her to be permanently shut up, however on this occasion I didn't think that having Paula killed was such a good idea. Why people liked to gossip was beyond my understanding. I couldn't afford for someone to link Paula's gossiping to her death. So Paula got to live.

I had to think of another solution.

The new Kate has been in hospital, unconscious, after being mugged during the time the other Kate had gone to the clinic. I couldn't quite remember why I had let her book herself into the clinic. What had I been thinking, it was a total waste of money, and now I had a bigger problem because of it.

Charles was long gone, and I hadn't heard from him since he'd left for Scotland. That had been intentional on my part.

Charles! The clinic that Charles had worked at would hold the records for Kate. Her cancer was on record, any doctor would probably have access to them.

I slammed my fist down on the desk, how could I have been so sloppy.

I picked up my mobile and dialled Pete. I tapped my fingers on the desk as I listened to the phone ring.

"H-e-l-l-o?" Pete's sleepy voice echoed down the line.

"It's Liam." I heard the rustle of fabric, the scraping of a clock and the thud as it was slammed down.

"It's four in the morning?" I wasn't sure if Pete was saying this because he thought I couldn't tell the time, or whether he was trying to indicate that I had rung at an inappropriate time.

"I don't care what time it is, I need you to do something for me."

"At four in the morning?"

"I'm not sure why the time is such an issue, we have a problem, I need some medical records deleting."

"I'm sorry?" Pete needed to wake up fast.

I sighed, because explaining myself was not in my nature. I expected people to do what I told them to do, no questions asked. "Kate had cancer, I want the records deleting, so that no one will find out that Kate is not Kate." Pete swore; I had finally got his attention.

I smiled for the first time since I had listened to Henry's message; Pete was going to delete the records for me. He stood to lose more than I did, and he knew it, because Pete was the mugger. If worse came to worse I could say that Kate had never told me about the cancer. The fact that the hospital treating the unconscious new Kate should have picked up on it, well, maybe it had been a wrong diagnosis. It wasn't as if she had got a second opinion. And, with the amnesia and everything, it wasn't like Kate was going to remember the cancer issue. Obviously, it would take a lot of explaining, and Pete would have to meet a rapid end, but I could do it. If worse came to worse.

I still had a chance to keep the new Kate. At this moment, she was oblivious to what was going on around her, as she slept in her bed, and Pete was going to make sure that it remained this way.

I gave him the clinic's address where Charles had worked. "And Pete, I want it doing straight away. Ring me when it's done, I don't care what time it is."

"Yes, Mr Thornton."

I hung up and paced round the room, my mind busy, I would ring Henry tomorrow, when I knew that Pete had destroyed the records, and explain that Paula couldn't have possibly seen Kate. Kate had been in hospital at the time, everyone knew that.

Why do people always believe the gossip, even, if, in this case it was founded?

It also didn't escape my notice that Paula had waited until Kate and I had left, before she had started gossiping.

Maybe Paula needed to learn a lesson.

I'd have to give that some thought.

Chapter Eleven

Kate

I kicked off my trainers and stopped the 'map-my-run-app'. I'd only had the time to run sixteen kilometres this morning. I was due to meet up with Jenny at eleven. I saved my run, looking at the split pace, six minutes six seconds per kilometre, not my best, but I had had things on my mind this morning.

Normally, when I ran my mind switched off, and I just enjoyed listening to the pounding of my trainers on the earth, and the music playing in my ears. Today my chest complained, and I'd had to strap my phone onto my left arm, all a reminder of what Liam had done to me last night.

I had lain awake for too long during the night, thinking, rather than sleeping. I recalled my conversation with Jenny about my lack of friends, at five this morning, it had occurred to me that Liam didn't have any friends either. He had business associates. Liam contained himself to himself, he trusted no one, and therefore he had no need for friends. Liam, being the controlling person that he was, would have ensured that I didn't make any connections and develop friendships. Friendships lend to people talking about themselves, and, well, I bet the last thing that Liam wanted was for me to discuss my life with him, with friends.

The more I thought about this, the more sense it made. I felt I was capable of making friends. I thought about Jenny, no, I had one friend, I corrected myself, it was just a shame that I would never be able to really talk to her about Liam.

Turning on the shower, I started to wash the sweat from my skin. Despite being awake for so long, I still hadn't worked out a way to rid myself of Liam. Liam had a lot of resources, and I knew that he would never just let me walk away from him. All this thinking with no solution was giving me a headache; I was stuck. There was no solution to my problem and it was eating at me.

Gently, I patted at my skin; the bruise on my chest looked angry, a purple stain on my caramel skin. It shouldn't be there. I wanted to cry, more from frustration than anything else. I would not let Liam abuse me in such a way again. I wouldn't – there wasn't going to a next time.

Thoughts darkening, I walked into the dressing room and selected a pale pink silk blouse with tiny blue, yellow and green flowers on it. It had a simple scoop neckline with a button at the back and soft pleating down the front, with little cap sleeves. The skirt I chose was a soft plain pink made from a heavier weighted silk. The skirt fell two inches short of my knees. Flat sandals would have looked just as good with the outfit as heels; however, it would appear that I didn't possess a pair of shoes without a heel. Picking up a pair of yellow kitten heeled sandals, I decided that these would have to do. They looked slightly more comfortable that the others.

I left my hair to hang down my back and dry in its own time, as I carefully applied my makeup. I looked at the bruise that ran down my arm. It was beginning to warm up out there, and I wasn't prepared to start wearing long sleeves or a cardigan to appease Liam. Nor was I about to slap makeup over it. It would only look false, and start to rub off, so what was the point. If Liam didn't like the bruise being on show, then he shouldn't have hit me in the first place.

Snatching the matching clutch bag to the shoes I threw in my phone, and a lipstick. Inside the bag was a small yellow purse. It was empty. I closed my eyes. OK, I needed money, and for that I would have to ask Liam. I wanted to bang my head against the wall, my frustration ran so deep. Instead, I let out a deep sigh and squared back my shoulders.

I went downstairs, looking first in the living room for Liam as I passed, before making my way to his study, heels clicking on the marble floor. I stood outside the door to the study wondering if I should knock, or just walk in. Better knock.

"Yes?" Liam's voice sounded from the other side.

I'd found him, so why didn't I feel happy.

I opened the door. "I'm just about to go into York and meet Jenny."

I watched Liam's eyes as they swept over my body, taking in the blouse and skirt, running down my legs to the sandals, assessing the lightly applied makeup, then to my slightly damp hair. Liam's eyes lingered on the bruise snaking along my arm. With a shrug of his shoulders he reached into the top drawer of his desk and took out his wallet. My back stiffened at his unspoken lack of remorse.

The room though large gave off a feeling of claustrophobia. The substantial mahogany desk was littered with papers. A telephone sat silently on the desk. It was old fashioned in appearance, with its square black body and clear plastic dial. A wall of books sat behind Liam, all of them leather bound. I was betting that each one of those leather-bound books would be first editions, and worth a fortune. The floor was mahogany, covered at one end by a Persian rug, where a black cast iron fireplace sat, framed by two large ox-blood leather wing back chairs. The window in this room was small, and deep red walls closed in around me. A

Rembrandt sat above the fireplace, far away from the window; I wasn't surprised to see it. I tried not to fidget. I didn't belong here; this was Liam's domain.

Liam threw a wad of notes onto the desk. "Jake Junior is taking the Aston Martin in for a service; he'll drop you off in town." Apparently, I would be getting a taxi back.

I picked up the notes and turned to leave. "Henry Henderson will be coming over on Monday, please make sure you make yourself available. Henry is bringing Jane and that kid of his with him."

I nodded my head and walked out the room, Liam was already sifting through the paperwork. Relief engulfed me as I closed the door on him.

Jake Junior was already sat in the car, when I walked out the front door. The smile on his face said that this was the stuff his dreams were made of. Jake Junior had yet to notice me, and I stood watching him, as he pretended to adjust a bow tie. Pulling at the sleeves of his clean blue overall, as though pulling down the sleeve of a tux, he checked himself out in the mirror. Not happy with what he saw, he raked his hair back from his face, giving himself a side parting. Sean Connery, Jake was not, with his red hair, but at that moment as he sat in the driver's seat of the Aston Martin, he was the best James Bond there had ever been in his head.

The moment passed as Jake Junior caught me watching him. Red stained his cheeks, but the smile on his face remained, as he quickly slid out of the car and ran around to open the passenger door for me. I smiled back at him amusement sparkled in the depth of my emerald eyes. It was the first time in a long time that I had forgotten my own problems, and allowed someone else's happiness to wash over me. "Mrs Thornton," Jake Junior said as he closed the door and ran around the other side. "Where would you like dropping off?"

I looked at Jake Junior as he happily gave the steering wheel a loving pat. "If you would drop me off outside the Minster, that would be fine," my smile broadened. "Before you do, why don't you take her for a spin down by the old Harrison estate? The place is empty and the road leading up to it has to be at least ten miles. Maybe you'd like to open up the engine and really see what she can do?"

Jake Junior's eyes lit up. We both knew that Liam would have a heart attack at the thought, but according to the log book the car was mine, and therefore I got a say. I saw the hesitation cloud Jake Junior's eyes. "Go for it Jake Junior, you may never get another opportunity." With that, he fired the engine to life and sedately moved the car down the drive, lest Liam was watching.

I was still smiling when Jake Junior dropped me off at York Minster. The tyres had squealed on more than one occasion as Jake Junior had taken a few tight bends, and we had both laughed and enjoying the ride as the Aston Martin's engine had opened up and sailed down the road at high speed. Now though the fun was over and the Aston Martin sat purring at the side of the road as Jake Junior came around and opened my door, extending a hand to help me out.

"Thank you, Mrs Thornton."

"I think I should be the one saying thank you. That was some driving back there." Jake Junior's face beamed, and I knew that for him, today would live on long after it had past.

I walked away and headed down High Petergate to meet Jenny. By the time I got there, Jenny already had several shopping bags. I was bang on time.

"What time did you start?" I asked eyeing the bags.

"Denis dropped me off on his way to work; I'm too fat to drive. The steering wheel keeps getting in the way of my bump."

I eyed Jenny. "Didn't you think of adjusting the steering wheel column?"

Jenny smiled and lifted her bags. "And what, miss out on getting in a bit more shopping." I shook my head and laughed at her.

Jenny wore a pale blue cotton maxi dress that accentuated her increasing breasts and bump. Her hair moved around her jawline as she laughed. A stab of jealousy hit me as I noticed the flat sandals on her feet.

"Here, give me your bags, this carthorse needs something to carry." Jenny laughed and handed over the bags.

I saw her face cloud over as she saw the bruise on my arm. "What happened?"

I looked at my arm. "It's nothing, come on the shops are open and there's money to be spent." Jenny laughed.

"So, where to now?" I asked as I rearranged the bags. They were mainly full of baby clothes so they weren't heavy, just cumbersome.

"Why don't we go for a drink? I could do with sitting down for a bit, my feet are beginning to swell."

Jenny led the way as we walked down the street to the Judge's Lodging. Taking a seat outside to enjoy the sun. I set the bags down onto the floor. "I need a pee," Jenny announced as I reached for my purse. "What do you want to drink and I'll get them in on my way?"

I put my purse away. "I'll have a latte, thanks." I watched Jenny as she waddled off into the pub.

I liked people watching, and I sat back in my chair enjoying the peace, as I lost myself to the people that walked by.

My eyes fell on a man in his early thirties. His black short hair was starting to turn grey at the sides. It suited him, giving him a dash of ruggedness.

He seemed familiar to me.

My interest spiked, as I moved my chair slightly to get a better look.

He was tall, at about six foot. He was a personal trainer, and it showed within the taut thick muscle of his arms and wide shoulders. Under the t-shirt was a perfect six pack my fingers itched to touch.

I took a breath, as my head caught up with what my body was saying. Why did I know he was a personal trainer? I questioned this as I watched him walk down the road in front of me. His swagger confident, the jeans pulling and stretching across his bum and thighs. Desire rose in me. I was very attracted to this man.

I looked back at his arms, and let out a breath of air. The memory of those arms circling round me as I sat on the kitchen floor, holding a glass of champagne shook through me. I took another look at the man in the distance, running my eyes down his body taking in the soft brown tint of his skin, and the red t-shirt that moulded itself to his chest. I licked my lips as my memory traced every outline of thick muscle that was hidden by clothing.

A child started crying and the man bent down and swung her up, long black hair cascaded down her back.

This was my child, my husband. I can't explain how I knew this, I just did. Unconsciously I twisted the rings on my left hand. Emotions of the past flooded my brain, they confused me. I'd seen the pictures in the wedding album that Liam had brought to the hospital. Everyone I'd met since knew me, and yet as I looked at the man in front of me, I knew I would never have left him, would never want to hurt him, by going off with another man, with Liam.

Liam wasn't worth leaving anyone for, despite his money. A shadow of pain was reflected in the man's deep blue eyes, and all I could think, was that it was there because of me.

Memories came rushing back.

I sagged in my chair, my head in my hands. I wasn't Kate.

I was Chrissie.

The name echoed round my head, as my daughter's tears dried up and she threw her arms round her daddy's neck, *my* husband's neck.

Wave after wave of memory came flooding back to me.

I stood up.

I needed to leave, to go back to Simon and my daughter.

My feet didn't move. I thought about how easily Liam had embedded me into his life. A flash of memory hit me, as I recalled a photograph that sat on the mantle at home.

My home, not Liam's.

It was of my twin sister and me, before I had been taken away.

I had vowed that one day I would find her. That we would once again be together as a family, as we were meant to be.

The thought sent me crashing down to my chair. I had become my sister. What had Liam done to her? I was Kate. It answered a lot of questions, as to why I didn't act the way Kate acted. My eyes widened as I recalled Liam's words, *"Why can't you be Kate!"* The answer was clear: I wasn't Kate.

Fear took me, what had he done with Kate? Had he killed her in a fit a temper? After what he'd done to me last night, I felt that he was capable of it. I thought back to when I'd been in hospital; Liam telling me about the mugging. I bet there had never been a mugging. Liam would have planned the whole thing. I'd been my sisters' perfect replacement; no one would have suspected a thing.

I was a fool, I should have known.

This life had never felt right to me, there had been a constant niggle in the back of my head.

Anger took me. My hands shook as I thought about what Liam had put me through, what he had put my husband through, what he had put my little girl through.

I'd go to the police; I'd get him locked up for this. His money wouldn't be able to buy him out of this.

The bastard would pay.

"*Kate! Kate!*" Jenny's urgent voice pressed against my consciousness. I turned to see her waddling towards me, her dress wet. "My waters have broken." Her eyes were wide with panic. There was a moment's hesitation, when all I wanted to do was run. Run to Simon, my husband, and throw my arms around him. I turned my head back to where I'd seen Simon, to find him gone. My heart gave a lurch. I closed my eyes; we'd be together again soon, I promised myself.

I turned to Jenny. "Don't panic." Which, was probably a stupid thing to say, to someone that was in the midst of labour, two months early.

Jenny shot me a look as though to say, like that wasn't going to happen. "Breathe," I said.

I took a deep breath with her, in and out, in and out.

"Oh God, it's happening, Kate I'm going to have my baby." I watched her face, as what she had said dawned on her. "I can't have my baby here."

I gave her a stern look. "You're not. The hospital isn't that far from here, I'll get a taxi or something." I looked around me. There was a taxi rank around the corner. I didn't think that Jenny would be able to make it that far.

The first contraction hit her.

A man stood up at one of the neighbouring tables. "My cars parked across the road, I can take you to the hospital."

I gave the man a grateful smile. "Thanks, that would be great."

I wrapped an arm round Jenny as she huffed next to me. I kept her standing; if she sat down I might not get her back up.

The man shrugged, picking up the shopping bags. "It's no problem, my wife had our first child in the supermarket. I know what it's like."

Jenny let out a breath and I looked at my watch timing the contractions as we slowly made our way to the man's car. I didn't think we had much choice, but to trust that the man wasn't a mass-murderer or something, praying on pregnant ladies.

The car rolled down the road, horn honking and lights flashing, as the man pulled right out in front of a car. "*Baby coming!*" The man shouted back to the other driver, who was displaying an array of hand jesters.

A policeman on a motorbike pulled up alongside us, lights flashing. "Don't worry ladies, the cavalry's here." I shot the man a worried glance; I wasn't so sure about that.

The man stuck his head out the window. "Baby coming," was all our driver said.

Jenny screamed and huffed in the back. The policeman nodded. "You'd better follow me." And like the sea had parted for Moses, so did the traffic and we suddenly had a clear path.

I reached into Jenny's bag, grabbed her phone and rang Denis. "Denis, you'd better come quickly, Jenny's waters have broken and we're on our way to the hospital." I hung up without giving Denis a chance to say a word. I didn't have time to enter into conversation. Jenny's contractions were getting closer together. This baby wasn't waiting for anyone.

"You're doing really well Jenny, we're nearly there." The hospital came into sight, and with a squeal of tyres we entered the hospital grounds.

People were waiting for us.

The policeman must have radioed it in.

A flurry of activity commenced as Jenny was assisted out the car and wheeled into the hospital. I'd just had chance to tell them that her contractions were coming in three-minute intervals. I nodded to our driver, and the policeman, throwing a relieved thank you over my shoulder as I followed Jenny and co into the hospital.

Jenny gripped my hand so hard that it felt like it was her personal mission to crush every bone in my hand. Denis wouldn't make it for the birth, and I wasn't about to leave Jenny, even if she was in good hands.

This was Jenny's first child, and she needed the support; the grip she had on my hand told me how much she needed me, more than words could.

"Relax, I'm here for the long haul," I said stroking her hair away from her sweat lined face.

"Thanks." Before Jenny could say anymore another contraction took hold and she screamed.

Chapter Twelve

Jessica

I looked at the little white and blue stick in my hand. The words on the little screen told me I was pregnant.

I looked down in the basket near the toilet and dropped the little stick into it. It clinked against the other six sticks that were there. Each stick telling me the same thing. I had wanted to be sure before I told Charles. After taking six tests, I was sure.

Giddy with excitement, I smoothed down my pale blue cotton summer dress and stepped out of the bathroom.

This was it, the moment I had dreamed of ever since Charles and I had come to Scotland. I knew Charles wanted kids; we'd talked about it on a few occasions. It had never happened with Liam. At first, Liam seemed unhappy about my not providing an heir to his fortune. He'd soon gotten over it, and had begun to view children as an inconvenience. Had we'd had a child, it would have ended up at boarding school, and brought out on special occasions to be paraded around and shown off. Liam was not a patient man, and children needed patience in abundance. As the years had gone past I begun to see my lack of conceiving as a good thing.

When Charles and I had started trying for a baby, I had been overjoyed at the prospect, however as the months had rolled by I had begun to panic, hence the six tests to confirm I was indeed pregnant.

I was going to have a baby.

Charles's baby.

I smiled.

Charles was at the clinic for another couple of hours, so I had time to prepare. I was on a mission to make the moment I told Charles about the baby as special as I could. I reached for the cook book; tonight, I would make Charles all his favourite foods. I began to sing to myself as I started cooking.

Within minutes the Kenwood Kitchen Aid was beating out a happy tune as it stirred the ingredients round, binding and mixing. I took the pastry that I'd prepared earlier out the fridge and stopped the mixer. I dipped a finger into the cake mix, hmmmm it tasted good. Pouring the mixture into a cake tin I set it in the oven, switching on the timer so I would remember to look at it. Turning, I began rolling out the pastry; the windows were open bringing in the song of birds.

I felt blissfully happy, and giggled to myself.

Ten minutes before Charles came home, I slipped into the bedroom and took out a pair of little white booties I had bought a few months back. I hadn't been able to resist them.

The front door clicked and I ran back into the kitchen, booties in hand, and hid them in a drawer.

"Something smells really good."

I smiled as Charles came into the kitchen. Eyes alight as he saw the steak pie coming out of the oven. "Mmm, so what have I done to deserve this?"

I laughed. "Oh Baby, this is nothing, you should see dessert."

Charles laughed and snaked an arm around my waist pulling me to him. "I can always have dessert first."

I pushed out of his arms. "Now, you know dessert is always best saved until last. Trust me; you're going to need the energy."

Charles reached for me again, and I slipped out of his reach. "Go get yourself into something more comfortable, foods served in ten minutes.

Charles smiled at me, a very wicked glint in his eyes. "Something more comfortable, hmmmm, I think I can manage that." He pulled at the tie round his neck.

I watched his retreating back, wondering what he was about to do. Charles had a definite wicked side to him, not that I was complaining, it certainly made things interesting.

Turning I began setting the table, humming to myself. Wiping my hands down my dress, which was now covered in flour, I gave the table another once over before reaching over for the pie. Turning to put it on the table I nearly dropped it on the floor, my mouth hung open as I looked at Charles standing by the kitchen door, *naked*.

He smiled at my reaction. "You did say comfortable." Yes, I had.

"Let's just hope you don't drop any gravy on your..." I looked down, "Well, just be careful."

Charles threw his head back and laughed at me, as he walked over grabbed me from behind, as I placed the pie down on the table. The fabric of my dress was thin and no protection against his roaming hands. "Stop it or tea's going to be served cold."

"I like cold pie." Hmmm, but not tonight.

I pulled away. "Sit, Romeo."

Charles pulled the chair out and sat down, as I put the mash potatoes, carrots and gravy on the table.

"This looks great, Jess." I beamed at the compliment; Charles liked his food.

"Tuck in before it gets cold." I reached for the pie and cut off a good size chunk for Charles.

"So, what did I do to earn this?" Oh Baby, you have no idea.

"I wanted to spoil my man."

"I like the sound of that."

I smiled, reaching across and kissing him. "So do I."

Charles tucked into the food on his plate, and I watched him, my bubble of happiness getting bigger and bigger.

Charles chatted about his day as we ate; his eyes alight as he told me that Robbie Jamison was going to make it. That was good news, Robbie was only fourteen. Robbie's mum, Janet, had been one of the first friends I had made here.

"That was delicious." Charles wiped his mouth with the napkin.

I moved across and took Charles's plate from the table. "I'm glad you liked it."

I cleared the table, not allowing Charles to do a thing to help. This was my moment. With a big smile, I reached for the white booties.

"Close your eyes." Charles wiggled an eyebrow at me, but did as I told him.

Quickly I set the little white booties in front of him. I bent down so that my mouth was close to his ear, and whispered. "This is what you did. Open your eyes."

Charles's eyes flew open, his eyes searching. I cocked my head to the table. He looked down and saw the booties. His mouth fell down and the biggest smile I'd ever seen lit his face with joy. I imprinted this moment to my brain, swearing I would never forget the look of sheer joy and wonder that crossed his face.

"This is…. This…is…it's wonderful." Charles grabbed me and I fell into his lap. A scream left my lips, before Chares covered them with a hungry kiss.

Breathless from the kiss I looked at him. "You're happy."

"No, happy doesn't cover it. You're wonderful, Jess."

"It was a joint effort."

Charles swung me up, "I love you."

My heart gave a flip. "I love you, too."

Charles lifted me away from the table. Leaving the kitchen, he carried me upstairs.

"What about dessert?" I asked.

"I'm just about to have it." I wasn't going to argue the point with him.

"This dessert bites back," I warned him.

Charles laughed. "I'm planning on it."

I giggled against his shoulder. I was so happy, so incredibly happy.

Chapter Thirteen

Liam

Something was wrong.

This was the fourth call that Kate had rejected from me. I knew that she was at the hospital with Jenny; Denis had rung to tell me. I had wanted to go, she was after all my sister, but work commitments prevented me. That's what I had told Denis.

In reality, the thought of sitting in the hospital waiting for a screaming baby to come into this world, was not my idea of being productive.

I picked up the phone that sat on top of my desk and started dialling. The ring tone shrilled out its call, and I tapped my fingers impatiently against the mahogany desk.

"Well?"

"She's just left your sister and brother-in-law," Pete's gruff voice filled the line.

"And?" I tried to contain my anger.

"She's leaving."

I wanted to slam the phone down on the desk and pretend it was Pete's head. "Then *stop* her, and bring her *here*." The man was incompetent sometimes, no independent thinking. I ended the call, leaving Pete stuttering to a dial tone.

I pushed away from the desk and wandered round the room. I couldn't shake the feeling that something was wrong. Kate should have picked up at least one of my calls at some point during the last four hours. I was beginning to wonder if she'd started to remember something about her past.

I recognised that the amnesia had been a flimsy plan.

If she had remembered something then I needed to step things up. I went back round to my desk and pulled out an envelope from the drawer. Maybe this would pull Kate in line. I smiled. I hadn't left anything to chance. I liked to think that I was the type of person that assessed a situation from all angles, and ensured that each one was covered, and to do that I had to have something that Chrissie treasured above all else; above her own welfare. I had just the thing.

I tugged the contents out of the envelope and looked at the photo of Chrissie's husband, Simon, and their daughter Imogene. These should be all the encouragement that Chrissie would need to leave her past behind, and stay, and do exactly what I wanted her to do.

I needed Chrissie gone, until all that remained was Kate, *my Kat*e. She was mine, she needed to know that. Needed to truly understand what that meant. If she didn't, well I hadn't quite decided which one I would have killed first, her husband or her daughter. Pete would not be happy, but then I didn't really care. Pete didn't really have a choice.

The way I saw it, either he did what I told him to do, or he'd be the one who'd end up in the dumpster, bleeding out.

Jeff Green was my usual hit man.

Jeff charged a lot of money.

He was a professional and very good at his job. Pete, however, needed to know who pulled the strings here. I was sick of his balking every time I asked him to do something, that didn't sit within his moral spectrum.

I had already put the hit out on Pete, one phone call and Jeff would pull the trigger, and then no more Pete. It would be a loss to my resources, but I'd replace him eventually.

Still, this didn't really have to happen, so long as Kate did as she was told. I put the photos back in the envelope as I heard the front door click shut.

Sitting back down at my desk, I shuffled through some paperwork. Seeing the photos had reminded me that I was still in charge; still in control of the situation.

I liked the feeling.

A knock sounded on the study door. I looked up at the door for a long moment, before answering the questioning knock.

"Come in." I put the papers down on the desk as Pete escorted Kate into the room. Flipping her hair over her shoulder, eyes smouldering with anger, she pulled her left arm out of his grip and walked away from him, setting a distance of about two foot between them.

"*Really Liam,* you didn't have to send the heavies in." Arms folded, she looked at me. There was a fire inside her that burnt near the surface. I looked forward to dampening that fire out.

"You didn't pick up any of my calls." I stared at her, as she rolled her eyes at me.

With a sarcastic laugh, she faced me. "And tell me Liam, out of interest just *who* were you calling."

I didn't like the new confidence that I saw in her, as she faced me. I felt the muscle in my cheek twitch. "You know who I was calling, I was calling you."

"Me? As in Kate?" I sat back in my chair, the bitch knew. I didn't know what had triggered her memory, I didn't care, I'd let her have her moment. "You see that's the problem Liam, I'm not Kate, and you bloody well know I'm not. Did you get your goon here to give me a good smack on the head? You must have been *sooo* happy when you found I couldn't remember anything. I'm betting that was your plan."

"Pete, leave us." I could see the relief on Pete's face as he turned to leave.

Kate turned. "Don't bother, I'm going."

Anger, pure hot, anger rose in me, as I looked at Chrissie, this was going to be the last time that I ever saw her in Kate. "I said leave, Pete." I pointed a finger at Chrissie. "You, you're staying right here."

"The hell I am. The thing is Liam, you can't make me."

She was so confident, so sure of herself. I smiled, this was going to be fun.

"I wouldn't be so sure about that, Kate."

Her eyes sparkled with anger. "*I'm not Kate!*"

"Get out!" I roared at Pete, who was stuck to the spot as though I'd super glued him there.

Squaring his shoulders, Pete left, closing the door behind him. I turned to look at Chrissie. "You're not as bright as you think you are, Chrissie."

Unease entered her eyes, with Pete gone I bet she'd thought she was safe. I almost laughed out loud at the thought. Reaching into the drawer I pulled out the envelope and threw it on the desk.

Chrissie eyed it with suspicion. "Open it. I'm sure you will find the contents very interesting."

She reached for the envelope. The photos dropped to the desk. A gasp left her parted lips. A series of emotions lighted her face, shock, fear, anger, resignation.

I smiled.

Pointing at the photos, I looked at her. I wanted to get my point across, make her understand exactly what I was capable of, of how far I was willing to go. "I can't decide which one should die first. Maybe *you* can help me with that."

Her eyes flew to mine, and in that moment, I saw realisation dawn on her face. She was mine, and there wasn't a thing she could do about it.

"You bastard," it was nothing more than a whisper.

I smiled at her, slow and sure.

I had won, again.

Now all that was left was for me to do, was to get rid of Chrissie, and for Kate to come back to me, for good.

I would break Chrissie's spirit, rip her apart.

I was quite looking forward to it.

Chapter Fourteen

Kate

I looked at the photos as they tumbled from the envelope. My blood ran cold; fear filled me and I began to shake. Simon's and Imogene's images floated before me. I looked at Liam. I believed him when he said he'd have them killed. Nothing stood between Liam and what he wanted. The amount of money he had, helped to bring his desires into fruition. I don't think that I had ever felt such complete and utter hatred for anyone, as I did for Liam.

Liam smiled; it was cruel and victorious.

He knew he'd won.

I picked up the photos and turned to leave the room.

"I'm not finished."

Slowly I turned, feeling like a fly caught in a spider web. I watched as Liam walked from behind the desk.

"What did you do with Kate?" I was shocked to hear my voice, faint and unsteady.

An ugly look crossed Liam's face. "She got cancer. No one leaves me, not until I say, and *she* got cancer." I closed my eyes; Kate had found a way out, albeit a permanent one.

I had missed my opportunity to ever see her again; pain stabbed at my heart cool and strong. She was my sister, my identical twin, a part of me felt as though I should have known that she had died.

I should have felt something.

Maybe if I had made more of an effort to find her, she may have been free of Liam sooner, and her last days on this earth wouldn't have been lonely ones. Life with Liam was empty, that man had no empathy for anyone.

Liam took hold of my arm.

I pulled away, instinct taking over.

His sharp blue eyes looked like two pieces of hard cold stone. It made me feel uneasy. "You've won Liam, I'm staying."

"It's not enough anymore." My eyes widened as he pulled at the neckline of my silk shirt. The shirt gave, the fabric parting exposing my flesh.

"*Get off!* I said you've won, I'm *staying*." I looked at Liam's face; he was resolute in his plans. "I'm not Kate, and nothing you can do will change that, *get off me!*" Fear ran through me. Nervously, I licked my dry lips as I looked at the solid wooden door; it was just out of reach. I'd never make it to the door in time. Two metres stood before me and freedom.

Two metres had never seemed so far.

The wind was knocked from my lungs as he pushed me to the floor. I scrambled away from him. There was no escape, nowhere to hide, in a room with little furniture and a poor excuse for a window.

Liam grabbed my right arm, pressing his fingers into the bruise. I couldn't stop the cry that came from my lips.

He smiled.

I hated feeling useless, fragile, breakable.

"You're wrong, once I've finished with you there will only be Kate." I swear my heart skipped a beat in fear.

"I can't be Kate, *I'm Chrissie!*"

A smile widened across Liam's lips. "No, you're Kate. You're mine."

I screamed as his hand ran up my legs and pulled at my knickers. The full impact of what he intended to do to me, made my heart pick up its pace; my brain recoiled at the thought. I began to fight him, kicking and thrashing about on the hard-wooden floor. I felt the draft as my knickers were pulled away.

"This is your problem. Kate was always more compliant."

"*I'm not Kate!*" I screamed. It left my throat feeling raw.

Liam didn't get it; how could I be someone I didn't know, that wasn't me. I could only be me. I hadn't seen my sister since I was nothing more than a little girl, with fanciful thoughts of princesses and unicorns.

I raised my left arm and swung a fist at Liam's head. It missed and struck his shoulder instead. He grunted but didn't stop. Liam's hand connected with my face. Fire warmed my cheek, where his hand had been. I screamed again, this time he hit me in the stomach, and I ended up coughing hard, as my lungs failed to fill with air.

"You are mine, the sooner you become mine, the easier it's going to be for you," Liam's voice hissed at me.

"I'll never be yours," I panted.

"I will break you." My skirt was wrapped around my waist, the lower part of me exposed and vulnerable. The shirt I had been wearing hung in two pieces, hanging on only by the arm holes.

I screamed again as Liam pulled down his trousers.

This was really going to happen, was the only thing I could think, and I closed my eyes trying to shut him out.

I screamed and screamed until my throat was sore, and the only noise I was capable of making was nothing more than a soft croak.

I fought Liam with everything I had.

It wasn't enough.

I had lost.

No, my brain echoed back at me, I hadn't lost. I could beat Liam despite what he had done to me.

My body felt sore and spent as I lay there. Liam removed his body off mine and a gentle breeze flitted across my exposed flesh. I opened my eyes to see Liam looking down at me, a satisfied smile on his face.

At that moment, I would have liked nothing more than to plunge a knife into his heart, and wipe that smile off his face.

"Get out." He turned his back, dismissing me.

Liam didn't have to tell me twice, I gathered the photographs from where they had fallen by the wing back leather chairs, and made my way to the door, pulling my shirt together. I didn't know where my knickers had gone. I wasn't going to spend the time looking for them.

Liam thought he had won; by this one act he thought he had broken me. I could see it in the satisfied way he zipped up his trousers and walked over to his desk, as though he had not just raped me.

I'd get him for this, I didn't know how, but I would.

Liam hadn't broken me, I was stronger than this. As my hands shook on the cold metal of the door handle, I kept reminding myself, I was better than this. I was stronger than this. I would not give Liam the satisfaction of thinking that by taking my body by force that I had become his victim. I told myself that I was only a victim if I let myself become one, and I wouldn't, *I wouldn't.*

I walked up the cold marble staircase, my heels clicking and clanking. I took off the sandals one by one, and threw them at the antique vase that sat on a table by the staircase below me. I screamed out my rage as the sandals left my grasp. One of them hit the vase and it tottered and fell, crashing to the floor.

The sound brought Liam scurrying from the study.

"You stupid bitch!" Anger made his face ugly.

"*I'm not Kate!*" I shouted back at him, and slammed the bedroom door behind me. The lock slid into place with a click.

No, I wasn't broken.

I looked down at the photos. "I'm so sorry, Baby." Simon smiled back at me, and I traced a finger over his face.

What did he think had happened to me? I thought about the sadness that had echoed in his eyes; tears fell down my face. Liam had put them there, and even if it killed me I would find a way to make him pay.

Placing the photos in the drawer of the bedside table, I stripped off what was left of my clothes. I looked at my naked body in the mirror. Bruises littered my body like a patchwork quilt. My cheek was red and a little swollen. The angry fire blazing in my emerald eyes, told me that my body might be beaten, but my spirit was still there.

Turning, I walked into the bathroom and turned on the shower; cold water sprang from the faucet and I scrubbed my body until it tingled.

I didn't cry, I didn't feel, and though my hands were unsteady, I was still me, Chrissie Sanders.

Not Kate.

Chapter Fifteen

Liam

I pulled at the white sleeves of my shirt, placing the cufflinks into the small slots at the cuffs, and tucking the tails of the shirt into my slim grey trousers. I wasn't due any meetings to today; still, I liked to dress smart.

I closed the door to Kate's room. It had taken three weeks, but I felt as though I was making progress. Today she had not fought me so hard; a few more days and she would be broken, and I would have my Kate back.

I never stopped to think about the person I had become. I enjoyed being me. You might be mistaken into thinking that something in my past had made me this way. The Thornton's were old money, and I'd grown up watching people take advantage of dad's 'good nature', wedeling themselves into his affections, and money, and had decided that no one was going to use me like that. I never stopped to think of the consequences that my actions had on others; so long as I won, I couldn't see a reason to be sorry. If I didn't win one way, I'd win another way. You'd be amazed how a simple drive in the county could be your last, or how easy it was to fall down the stairs to your death. Jeff Green was very inventive. Each one had been labelled as an *'accident'*. Yep, Jeff was definitely worth his one million a hit price tag.

I could hear Kate banging about behind the door. Maybe I should give it another week. *My* Kate had never shown such spirit. I found it frustrating.

I'd had to move Henry Henderson's visit back by a month. I couldn't very well invite him and his ugly wife, and even uglier kid here with Kate looking as she did. The bruises would take a few more days to go.

I had let my temper get the better of me. I had realised that when I'd seen the bruise that had lined her cheek. Since then I had made sure that any damage done, could be covered by clothing.

Appearances, it was all about appearances.

My mobile rang. I looked at it, it was Pete. I put it back into my pocket. The man was becoming a liability. I was sick of hearing his constant whinging about Kate. That was the thing about Jeff Green, he never whinged, so long as he got paid on time, there was no problem.

I began to walk down the marble steps to my office, it was about time that Pete and fate had a chat, and I knew just the man.

"Hello!" Jenny's voice rang from the hall.

A baby's cry went through me.

Why people felt the need to have them was beyond me. They were like a chain around your neck, tying you down, and draining your finances.

What the hell was she doing here? I swallowed back my irritation as I stopped halfway down the stairs, turned and went back to Kate's room.

Opening the door, I noticed that the bed was empty. The running of water drew me to the bathroom. I opened the door. Kate froze mid step into the shower. I looked over the bruises that littered her body, across the tops of her arms and upper thighs, along her breasts and stomach. The ones on her chest and stomach were the worse.

I congratulated myself; once dressed, even with three quarter sleeves, no one would be able to see the bruises.

Kate eyed me with suspicion. "Jenny's here, make sure you put on some makeup." She didn't move, just stood there waiting for me to leave. "Put some trousers and a shirt on, I don't want you upsetting Jenny." I smiled inwardly to myself as I saw Kate's eyes blaze with anger.

Power, it was all about power. By telling Kate what to wear I was stamping my authority over her, and she knew it. I liked the feeling. Chrissie may still be putting up a fight, but I was still winning, in the end she'd see that, and become *my* Kate.

Turning, I closed the door behind me and left the room.

Jenny was half way up the stairs, her maxi skirt swishing against the marble steps. The top she wore, I thought, was unflattering for a woman who was big breasted, and still clearly carrying a lot of post baby weight. The fitted vest top was a light peach colour that went well with the varying shades of pink and gold of the skirt, highlighting the rosy tint to her cheeks.

While I felt the need to point out to Jenny that with no makeup on she looked very homely, I didn't. If I had, I would have also let her know that her hair needed tending to. Unlike Kate, Jenny could not leave her hair unattended. It currently resembled a dried-out bird's nest.

I met her halfway up the stairs, and steered her back down, baby resting against her chest. The pink clothing depicted the baby's gender. All babies looked androgynous; hence a parent's need to clothe their babies in a gender-related colour.

Jenny and Denis had decided to call their baby Elsie after our own dead mother.

Ten years after our parents had died, rather suddenly in a car accident, along a country road, and Jenny still mourned their loss.

That had been the first job that Jeff Green had done for me.

Our parents' death had been one of my first triumphs; it had shaped me into the man I was. I didn't regret my decision. They had become too interested in my business plans, and failed to listen to the many warnings I had given them. Their funeral had been a lavish affair, and I had secretly congratulated myself on how well it had all gone.

With death came freedom, and I don't mean for those that died. I mean for the people they left behind.

It was a shame that Jenny would never be able to see things my way. She was too much like Mother, too sweet and nice, always thinking of others and trying to please. Jenny's only saving grace was that she didn't poke her nose in where it didn't belong. It allowed her to continue to live.

"Why don't you settle yourself in the conservatory and I'll get Mrs Jones to bring in some refreshments. Kate won't be too long, and I have some business that needs attending to. You look well, Jenny." I sounded insincere, what did she expect turning up here looking like she did.

I placed a light kiss on her forehead and left the room in search of Mrs Jones.

Mrs Jones was a stocky woman, with dyed dark brown hair that didn't suit her pale complexion or age. In her late fifties, Mrs Jones was not a beauty, her features were too sharp and her jaw line too masculine. Her hair had turned white early on, and the white roots that sprung between her parting line, where the dye had outgrown, only made her look older. Lines ravaged her face due to too many years of smoking. So, long as she didn't smoke while at work it didn't bother me. I even overlooked the smell of smoke that clung to her, and lingered in the rooms she had recently vacated. I chose to ignore this only because Mrs Jones was good at her job. She knew when to be seen, and when to remain hidden from view. The house was always tidy and the food good. She also knew how to keep her mouth shut.

Mrs Jones had worked for me ever since the death of my parents. I had got rid of everyone else. Everyone that was, but Jake.

Jake, was the only thing I had kept of my childhood. I had spent too many years talking to him as a boy over the roses, while he mowed the lawn or worked in the greenhouse. Jake had never criticised my choices.

Jake was my only indulgence. There was no logic to this indulgence; I only knew that for some unexplainable reason I could not, and would not let Jake go. The thought of losing him was inconceivable. It was a weakness that I could not seem to let go of, and so I chose to ignore it, which is why I had employed Jake Junior.

The soft tread of footsteps sounded on the marble floor and I stopped midway to the study as Kate descended the stairs. Kate was a rare beauty, with her long silken hair and soft almond-shaped emerald eyes. Her caramel skin glistened against the soft cream shirt that hugged at her waist and billowed out in soft thin pleats on the sleeves. The pale blue trousers she wore defined the long slim length of her legs. The cream spiked sandals gave her an extra two inches.

A smile curved her lips as she caught the sounds of a gurgling baby.

I stood transfixed as I watched her make her way down the stairs; she was a vision, and she was all mine.

I turned and walked into my study, softly closing the door behind me.

Chapter Sixteen

Kate

The bathroom door opened and Liam stood there, Armani shirt in place and trousers smoothed out. He looked irritated. The focus of his irritation couldn't be me, and I didn't think that even Liam, could have enough energy for a second round. My hand made a fist at my left side, hidden away from his sharp blue eyes, as he stood there taking in the bruises that littered my body.

My emotions were all over the place.

Since the incident in the library Liam had come for me every day, beating and raping me. I had noticed a change in the areas where he hit me. I knew that it was because of what he'd done to my face.

A trophy can't be shown off to its optimum if it's damaged.

I was beginning to understand Liam, and what drove him, all too well. I liked to think of it as research, because at some point I would have enough information on Liam to get a plan together that would set me free.

I stood, not moving as Liam's eyes met mine.

I didn't look away.

There was no way that he was going to break me. The words had almost become a singsong in my head, each time that Liam abused me, they rattled round and round; *'I will not be broken, I'm Chrissie; I will not become Kate'*.

"Jenny's here, make sure you put on some makeup." I wanted to punch him. "Put some trousers and a shirt on, I don't want you upsetting her." Liam turned and left, closing the door.

I couldn't stop the shaking that had my knees knocking and my hands unsteady as I wiped the hair from my face. *'I will not be broken, I'm Chrissie; I will not become Kate'*.

The water stung as it hit my skin. I scrubbed Liam from my body, wishing I could so easily scrub him for existence. Hair shampooed and conditioned I turned off the shower and gently patted my skin dry.

Reaching for the bottle of Argon oil I smothered it over my body, watching it sink in. Sighing, I walked from the bathroom and into the dressing room, giving the oil chance to soak completely into my skin before adding perfume and deodorant.

I viewed the clothes that lined the racks in the dressing room. Reaching, I pulled a cream shirt off the hanger and threw it onto the padded bench. Pale blue trousers followed the shirt. The bra I put on pressed against the bruises across my chest and breasts. Angrily, I swiped at the tear that ran down my cheek. I hadn't even known I'd been crying until I'd felt it run down my face. My eyes suddenly stung, and I clenched my hands. I would not cry. To cry would be to let Liam win, and I couldn't, no wouldn't, allow him the satisfaction.

Angry at myself, I dressed quickly, and applied the makeup that Liam had told me to wear. I closed off my mind, running a tune round my head to stop me from thinking.

If I didn't think, then I didn't feel, and if I didn't feel, well, I could survive this.

I closed the door to the bedroom the lock had been removed the day after I'd confronted Liam. The day my memory had come back to me.

My heels sang out a happy tune, in beat to the tune that I sang in my head. It was Imogene's favourite nursery rhyme, *'The Grand Old Duke of York'*. She liked it because it had York in the title, and we lived in York.

I heard the soft gurgle of Elsie as I came down the stairs; a soft smile curved my lips. A sound of innocence, of happiness and contentment, in my world of coldness and brutality. Jenny was a great mum. I followed the sound of Elsie's soft voice into the conservatory. Mrs Jones was laying out a tray filled with coffee, tea, and biscuits. She wore a tight black dress that seemed to make her shoulders appear wider. Thick legs poked out from beneath the respectable knee length hemline. Her hair was ready for dyeing again, judging by the length of white roots on display. I didn't understand the obsession she had with using such a dark colour, when her hair was so obviously white. It made maintenance a nightmare.

I didn't like the woman; she smelled heavily of smoke, and always seemed to look down her nose at me, as though I was trash. She had no idea of who the real trash in this house was.

Ignoring Mrs Jones, I walked over to Jenny and held out my hands. "Come on Elsie, let your favourite auntie have a hug." Jenny beamed and Elsie gurgled happily as I took her into my arms.

"You're a natural," Jenny smiled up at me as I balanced Elsie in my arms and cooed at her. "I think I worry too much."

"All new mums worry, it's a very natural thing. You're doing a great job, Jenny." I sat down next to her, as Elsie blew a bubble at me.

"Do you think Liam and you will ever have kids?" I blinked at Jenny, stunned by the question. Even though it was a natural question to ask, the thought of a little Liam running around, was, well, it was not something I wanted to think about. It sent shivers rippling down my spine.

"I don't think Liam's work would allow him the space for kids." I congratulated myself for being diplomatic. None of this was Jenny's fault, and I had vowed that I wouldn't take it out on her. Jenny was not Liam, in fact she was one of the nicest people I had ever meet, and that meant a lot to me.

Jenny gave me a little frown. "It just seems wrong; you're so good with Elsie. You'd make a great mum." I wanted to tell Jenny that I already was a mum, that I had a beautiful daughter. That Simon and I had talked about having another baby.

The thought made me sad. Simon and I would never have another baby, and Imogene would never know how much her mummy really loved her. My eyes filled with tears and I blinked them away, as I softly breathed in the smell of baby powder.

Jenny's hand laid softly on my arm. "I'm sorry Kate, I didn't mean to pry. Sometimes I think Liam doesn't have his priorities in order." Poor Jenny, she thought that my not having children was Liam's fault because of his work commitments. If only she knew.

I smiled at her. "Now that's enough of that, you didn't come here to talk about me and Liam. You came to show off this wonderful little girl of yours. And so, you should, she's positively beautiful, just like her mum."

Jenny beamed and a little self-consciously smoothed her down her hair. "She is beautiful, isn't she? It's strange, but I don't think I truly knew what love really was until Elsie screamed her way into the world. Not that I don't love Denis, of course I do, it's just this love I feel for Elsie, why I would do anything in my power to ensure her happiness. It's almost scary."

I jiggled Elsie in my arms, freeing a hand. I laid a hand on Jenny's. "Welcome to motherhood. Children are special; it's why we love them so much."

Jenny sighed and I handed a wiggling Elsie back to her. "I think she's getting hungry."

"I only fed her a couple of hours ago."

"I don't think Elsie can tell the time yet, and right now she wants feeding." Elsie puckered up her lips and graced us with a cry of hunger, as though agreeing with me. Jenny laughed and took Elsie from me.

"She's just like her mum, I'm always hungry too."

"In that case, I should be a better hostess and pour you a cup of tea, and if we leave those biscuits any longer, I reckon they'll go soft and won't be worth eating."

Jenny looked at me. "You're the best, Kate."

Elsie latched onto Jenny's breast and contented little sucking noises echoed round the room.

Chapter Seventeen

Jessica

I had been sitting on the cold tiled floor for about an hour or so now, staring into the toilet. Morning sickness had hit me three weeks ago. I wiped at my mouth slowly, reaching for the sink and pulling myself up. Swilling water round my mouth, I spat the acid taste of sick away. Why they called it morning sickness I don't know, because I was fine in the morning, it was in the afternoon that the waves of sickness hit me.

I smoothed down the front of my summer dress, its bright yellow fabric, was a good deal sunnier than I felt. The front door clicked and I heard the soft tread of footsteps on the stairs. Charles didn't have to look too far at the moment to find me. I sank back down onto the cold tiles and took a deep breath, not finished yet.

The blue denim hem of Charles trousers appeared next to me and warm hands pulled the hair out of my face as I gripped the toilet. Not the most romantic image that I ever saw for us, still I was grateful that Charles was here. A glass of cold water dangled in front of me and I took it, spitting the contents out into the toilet. We sat in silence for a few minutes, each of us trying to gauge if the sickness was over for another day.

"Do you feel like you can move yet?"

Right now, speaking took up too much energy, especially as I was assessing how I felt, and more importantly, if I could now leave the bathroom. I nodded my head to indicate that I thought things were settling down. Charles gently scooped me up and I leant against his chest, the soft fabric of his burgundy t-shirt rubbed against my cheek.

Charles carried me downstairs and sat me on the sofa, my legs fell across his lap, as my bottom sank into the feather cushions. The sofa was too big for the room, but it enabled us both to comfortably stretch out on an evening, so I didn't care. The check red fabric complemented the curtains that hung by the large window. I leant into the crook of Charles' arm, as he handed me a packet of dry crackers. I seized the crackers and began munching; I'd found that they helped settle things down.

Charles's hand rested protectively on my tummy, I smiled as I munched. My bump wasn't big, just a gentle swell. I loved it, every tiny inch of it. It was a reminder of our love, and what we had created together. I wasn't that far on that I felt uncomfortable, still I was reaching my third trimester, and that was a big milestone for me. Everything was going well, and I just couldn't believe that this was really happening. I was here with Charles, having our first baby, and I was happy, so incredibly happy, that it just didn't feel real at times.

"I think I'll have to get some new clothes soon, things are starting to get a little tight," I said around a mouthful of crackers, indicating my slightly swollen belly with a small incline of my head.

Charles' hand rubbed gently across my stomach, "Why don't we go shopping on Saturday?"

"Sounds good, we'll need to get an early start, I don't fancy throwing up in the public toilets." Charles chuckled softly.

"Oh, I think I can manage that, early to rise early to bed." There was a wicked glint in his eyes, and I laughed softly into his chest.

"Don't you think that, that's what got me in this position in the first place?"

"There's nothing wrong with the position that you're in, in fact, I can definitely see benefits to it."

Charles moved his hand from my stomach and traced it along the tops of my thighs, sneaking under the skirt of my cotton dress. My breath caught as his hand ran slowly and tantalisingly up my leg. The crackers I was holding fell to the floor as I reached for Charles's hand. My eyes caught the headlines of the newspaper Charles had left on the coffee table that sat next to the sofa. *'Tycoon Files for Bankruptcy.'* I grabbed the paper, looking at the photo of Henry Henderson.

'Profits slumped for Henderson Corp, when a vicious takeover by Sitcom Industries caused stocks to plummet. Self-made tycoon Henry Henderson was left desolate, as his wife left him, following the death of their son Jamie from a heart defect...'

My hands trembled, why had Liam done it?

"What's wrong?" Charles grabbed the crumpled newspaper, opening it, his face paled as he read the article.

"Sitcom Industries is one of Liam's offshore business. I wonder if Henry knows." I paused as I considered this. "No, I doubt it; Liam's relationship with the company is buried pretty deep."

I looked across at Charles. "Why does he have to do it? It's not like Henry was hurting anyone. I just don't understand."

"I don't know. Liam has changed so much that I don't even recognise him anymore." Charles folded the paper and placed it back on the coffee table, pulling my legs with him as he lent back against the sofa. "He can't hurt you anymore, Jess."

I smiled at him and gently laid a hand on his tanned cheek. "I know Baby, it just makes me sad, when I see the destruction Liam can bring, and for what? Because Liam doesn't like self-made money, I'm not quite sure why."

"Come on," Charles swung my legs off the sofa, reaching for my cream cardigan. "Let's go for a walk to the beach."

I smiled at him; Charles didn't like it when I was sad. "I'll only go, if you promise not to throw me in the sea."

"I didn't throw you in the sea, as I remember, I was piggy backing you, and you followed me into the sea."

I put a finger against Charles's chest. "You, mister, are not that innocent." Charles opened his hazel eyes wide in innocence, before that mischievous glint appeared.

"Hey, if you want wicked, why didn't you say so." I let out a scream as Charles swung me up into his arms, carrying me through to the kitchen and picking up the picnic blanket as he made his way outside.

"You know there are advantages to living so close to a quite unpopulated beach. And I intend to explore every one of them."

Charles dropped my feet to the ground, I wasn't wearing anything on my feet and the grass tickled my toes. "Oh, you do, do you? Well, in that case I'll race you there. First one there gets to explore their creative talents on the other one first." I leapt away into a long stride.

Charles swore at my swiftness and came for me like a bull spotting a patch of red cloth. I laughed and increased my pace. Running was my thing; it had got me through an awful lot of bad times with Liam. It had allowed me to stop thinking, and to just listen to the soft pounding of my feet as they hit the ground. Now as I ran, I was thinking about all the creative ways I was going to make Charles scream my name, over and over again, by the time I'd finished with him. The thought got my feet moving faster, my breath catching in my throat, a smile on my face.

Chapter Eighteen

Liam

I threw down the newspaper; the headline caused a smile to twitch at the corner of my lips, *'Tycoon Files for Bankruptcy'*. I recalled the day that Henry Henderson had come here into this very study to sign the contract. The contract had given me access to Henry's company, and I had wasted no time in splitting the company up and providing Sitcom Industries with the resources for a hostile and swift takeover.

Henry Henderson had sat in the leather-bound wing back chair at the end of the study, swivelling his whisky round his glass, watching the ice clink together as he had given me a considering stare. I'd stared right back, I knew that Henry would sign the contract; he didn't really have much of a choice, due to a couple of bad investments. Those investments had lined my pockets well. It was amazing how easy business dealings could be sometimes, but then Henry didn't have an appreciation of money and the power it held. That was the problem with self-made- money.

Henry's suit had been two sizes too small for him; the thick creases at the stitching distorted the deep grey pinstripe as it puckered under the stress. The white shirt he wore was open at the collar, his blue tie dangling across his chest. I curled my lips in distaste as I smoothed the fabric of my trousers along my thighs. The navy fabric lay in a soft fold as it should. My blue striped shirt was fastened at the collar and the dark blue silk tie sat straight at the shirt collar. If you were going to undertake a business deal it was important that you were dressed as refined as the contract on the table.

Henry may purchase at the top end of the fashion market, but he was in denial, not only about his actual size, but about his worth. The man inside the suit was not worth the sophistication of the cut of the cloth, or the price tag that went with it.

Jane's shrill voice carried down the hall through the slight gap in the study door. I'd purposely not closed it. Jane was loud and that awful child of theirs even louder. I had wanted to remind Henry that this business deal was all he had left, if he wanted to hang onto his company. The thought had made me laugh inwardly, because within a month of signing the contract, Henry would be back where he belonged with the riffraff trash, who were known as middle-class.

Even the title they gave themselves prevented them from ever achieving anything real. And, well, even if they did, like Henry had done, there was always someone like me waiting, and ready to take it from them, bringing them back down to where they belonged.

Henry smiled at the sound of Jane's voice, which was being quickly followed by Jamie's. The door to the study flew open banging against the wall. I tried not to show my irritation as the brat ran into the study.

"Daddy, Daddy, can we go now, I want to ride Butch." That pony of Jamie's was anything but butch. Butch was a shabby brown Shetland pony, which Henry had bought on a whim to make Jamie happy. That boy was too much like his father to truly appreciate anything.

Henry smiled at Jamie. "You know, Daddy has some business to do, why don't you go out in the garden with Mummy and Kate."

Jamie's lips puckered into a sulk. "They're being boring, and talking nonsense."

Henry chuckled. "That's women for you, son."

I had begun to think that the brat would ruin everything. "Why don't you ask Kate to take you to see Jake?" The kid had pouted. I had sighed. "Jake has had lots of adventures. Why don't you ask him about the time that he was kidnapped by some Russians?"

Jamie's face puckered some more as he gave this some thought. "Were they real Russians?"

"As real as you and me." I had smiled encouragingly at the kid to get him to leave. Jake had told me the story about the Russians when I had been Jamie's age. Not that I thought the story held any truth to it, I didn't, however it was a very good story. One a small boy would enjoy.

The thought of the Russians was enough, and Jamie had turned to leave. "*Kate! Kate! Kate!*" The kid had a good set of lungs on him.

The clicking of heels brought Kate in our direction. I gave her a cool look as she entered the study. I'd been pleased to see that I hadn't had to say anything; my Kate was coming back to me. I leaned back in my wing back chair opposite the one Henry sat in, feeling rather satisfied with myself.

I watched Henry as his eyes travelled down Kate's body. Her long lean legs were on show, in a pair of white tailored shorts and sky blue halter neck top. Her hair was up in a high ponytail. Normally, I would have had a cutting comment to make about such a simple, common style, however today it highlighted her slim shoulders, and ran down her bare back in a loving caress.

I had coughed at Henry, as he'd checked out Kate's rear, bringing the man's eyes back in my direction. The door softly closed behind Kate and the singing kid, that was chanting "Russians, Russians" over and over again.

"Henry?" I indicated the contract that sat on my desk, with a nod of my head.

"Of course." Henry pushed himself from the chair and waddled over to the desk.

I remained where I was. I had already signed the contract, and I didn't want Henry to know how important this was to me. So, I swivelled my own whisky around my glass and watched as Henry plucked the pen from his shirt pocket and placed his scrawl on the contract. Victory was mine again, and I had thrown back the contents of the whisky glass, enjoying the burning as it had tricked down my throat.

Chapter Nineteen

Kate

I ran across the lawn towards the house; sweat trickled down my back and my breath came in an even rhythm. I slowed down as I approached the patio area, and the steps that led up to the back of the house, and began stretching out. Jake paused from the rose bush he was deadheading, and began wandering over to me. His old body made slow progress as his left leg limped stiffly from the arthritis that ate at his bones. I sat down on the steps and turned off the music, flipping to *'map-my-run-app'*. I paused the app and saved my workout. I'd run 20.43 kilometres today. I sighed, the run had done my body good but my mind was still too active, for me to enjoy it like I normally would have. *Bloody Liam.*

"Morning, Jake," I called over my shoulder as the soft shuffle of his footsteps came closer.

Jake came to stand at the base of the steps; I looked up at him, shading my eyes from the sun with my right hand. "You're not Kate, are you?"

The colour drained from my face as I looked at Jake. His wrinkled old face was scrunched up in thought as he waited for my response. From the knowing glint in his eyes he already knew the answer to the question. He was just looking for confirmation. I dreaded to think what Liam would make of this. That said, I couldn't see the point in lying to the old chap.

I sighed, guilt and tiredness making their voices heard in that one deep sigh. "No, my name is Chrissie, I'm Kate's twin sister. Liam said that Kate got cancer." My throat tightened up, I couldn't bear to say that Kate was dead, that I should have made more of an effort to find her, while I'd still had the time.

The rustling of fabric and clicking of old joints came from my right as Jake lowered his old weathered body down beside mine. The soft worn green cords pulled at the knees where brown patches had been sewn on each leg of the trousers. Jake pulled at the pocket of his blue polo shirt, as he removed a small piece of paper. "Kate never had cancer."

I looked up at him, hope shined in my eyes; if she had never had cancer, she would still be alive. She'd found a way to get out, to get away from Liam. I was no longer in a position to find her, not with Liam around. He was already threatening to have my daughter and husband killed; I didn't want to think what he would do with Kate if he knew she was still alive.

"Kate, is living with that doctor of hers." Jake's voice roused me from my thoughts. "She thought no one knew, but Kate couldn't hide the truth from me, I'd seen the way they looked at each other." Jake smiled in thought. "She deserved to be happy. I told her that when she left. I'd always known that she'd find a way to make things work, that she had finally found the peace and happiness that Liam couldn't give her." Jake looked at me, a soft glaze of tears washing out the colour of his eyes. "Why'd you take her place?"

I looked down at my hands; they rested on the black and pink three quarter running pants. "Liam found out about me, I don't know how, but I'd bet it had to have something to do with that thug of his, Pete Townsend. After the amnesia cleared, well, by then it was too late." I tried to hide the bitterness from my voice, but I was through pretending, and with Jake, I'd apparently found someone I could talk to. Be myself with.

"I hate him, Jake. I never thought I could possibly hate someone the way that I hate Liam, and there's nothing I can do. I'm stuck here. He knows about my daughter and husband. He said that he would have them killed if I didn't become Kate." Jake's hand rested across my shoulders.

I turned and cried into his chest, my chest heaved and my sobs engulfed my body as it shook to the rhythm of my hiccupped breath. "Shh, shhh, lass there's always a solution to most things; we just have to find one." Jake's breath cooled the back of my neck, and I breathed in the earthy smell that clung to him.

"I don't know how to stop him Jake. Look at what Liam did to Henry Henderson. He ripped that poor man's life apart, and Henry doesn't even know that it was Liam who did it. I know though. I don't know how Liam did it but he did. Henry has lost everything, his kid, his wife, his home. I can't afford for that to happen to those that I love, that Liam has forced me to leave behind." I blew into the hanky that Jake handed me.

I looked up into Jake's weathered face. "How did you know?"

Jake smiled at me, handing me a small piece of paper. I unfolded it, to find a photograph of Kate and me when we were kids. We were about five in the photograph. Our arms were clasped around each other in a hug, our heads touching as we smiled happily at the camera.

"She asked me to keep this safe for her. I think she was afraid that Liam would find it." My eyes filled with tears again as I looked at the old photograph, with our pretty pink identical dresses and ribbons in our hair. Even for me it was difficult to see the differences between us. It was the eyes that set us apart; Kate's were soft full of hope and dreams, whereas mine held the hard edge of stubbornness. Even then, Kate was the one that would comply, would go out of her way to make others happy.

"No two people are alike. Not everyone can see through the outside of a person, to where the main differences are kept. I can. You may look like Kate, but I see the differences." I looked at Jake as he spoke. With a pang of sorrow, I handed him the photograph back. He took it and carefully folded it, placing it back into its hiding place. Jake patted the pocket as though reassuring himself that his little secret was safe.

Jake Junior came around from the side of the house carrying a spade over his left shoulder. I could hear him singing to himself as he jaunted round to the beat of his song. Jake Junior was like a little songbird, an out of tune songbird, but you couldn't have everything; his happy mood was infectious. I wiped the last of the tears from my eyes, a smile played across my lips as Jake and I watched his approach.

Unlike Jake, Jake Junior wore a blue overall that still had that stiff new fabric look to it. I stood. "I'd better go. Thanks, Jake."

Jake looked up at me and smiled gently. "I don't know what he thinks he's going to dig up, but whatever it is I'd better go save it." I laughed as Jake pushed his body away from the steps and shuffled over to Jake Junior, who by the look of it, was well aware of what Jake was going to say about the spade, a playful smile lit his lips as he stopped and watched the old man hobble over to him.

Slowly, I walked towards the house. A wave of sickness suddenly struck me, and I clutched my stomach and ran the last few yards into the house, to the downstairs cloakroom. Most people's cloakrooms were a small affair, not Liam's. The toilet sat against the back wall and I dropped down next to it raising the lid, discounting the large white matching sink, and gleaming deep oak cupboard that an antique vase sat on, or the expensive painting that probably cost more than most people could earn in a lifetime. The painting was by an up and coming artist, and it showed what Liam thought of it, that it hung in the downstairs cloakroom.

"Kate!" Liam's voice echoed down the hall. He sounded annoyed. Right now, I didn't care, as I laid down on the white tiled floor.

Another wave of sickness struck me, as Liam walked through the door. The look of disgust on his face spoke louder than any words could. I wanted to cry again, as I threw up into the toilet. I hadn't felt this bad, this suddenly, since I'd fallen pregnant with Imogene, and the thought struck a chord of recognition in my head. My periods had never been regular and with everything that had been happening lately, I'd never put too much thought into when my last period had been. Now as I gazed down at the toilet, all I wanted to do was take back the realisation that I was pregnant, *pregnant* with Liam's child.

I threw up again, this time the tears that stung the backs of my eyes fell down my face. Liam hadn't moved, but I could tell that my being sick was becoming an inconvenience. *Wait* till he found out I was pregnant.

"Kate!" Irritation laced each letter of my sister's name, as I sank to the tiled floor. "The marquee people are here, I need you to organise them." I wasn't going anywhere right now.

With a lot of effort, I peeled my upper body off the tiled floor and sagged against the wall; my movements were slow and a little unsteady. "Sorry, Liam, I'm a bit busy at the moment." I lifted a hand to point at the toilet.

"Well, I can't do it; I have more important things to do." I cracked my right eye open and looked at him.

"Seriously Liam, it's not going to happen." As if on cue my body heaved and I slumped over the toilet.

I heard Liam take a step back. "What's wrong with you?" The lack of care or warmth in Liam's voice chilled me.

I moved gently back against the wall. "Oh, I'll tell you what the matter is, Liam, I'm pregnant, and that's what's wrong here." Liam's face paled slightly. "I bet you never took that into consideration while you were raping me night, after night."

"I did not rape you, you're my wife."

I cocked a brow at him. "No, Liam we both know that that technically isn't correct. I'm actually your sister-in- law. You know, the one that you and your thug knocked down some stairs and claimed as yours. And by the way, even if I was your wife, no still means no, and rape is still rape."

Liam went to hit me, my body convulsed. He took a step back, clever boy. I leaned forward and faced the toilet again.

"You're going to have to get rid of it." Liam's words hit me as I emptied the last of the contents of my breakfast.

Moving away from the toilet I looked at Liam, as he stood there in his Armani black striped suit and off-white shirt, gold silk tie and Gucci shoes. He cut a nice picture, if you didn't mind the ice cold blue eyes. "I'm not about to kill an innocent baby, even if that child is yours." Until that moment I hadn't realised how I felt about this baby. It wasn't the baby's fault that its father was a cold, unfeeling bastard. Life was life to me.

"You will get rid of it, Kate." Liam's voice cut into me, slicing like ice. I made the decision not to reply and threw up into the toilet instead.

When I came back up Liam had gone and I slumped down onto the cold tiles in relief. I decided that I'd lay here for another half hour or so, to make sure the sickness wave had passed before making my way upstairs.

The marquee Liam had referred to was for the charity event he had arranged. Well, he had arranged it, so it was only fair that he did all the organising as well. As it was, he should be glad that I was going to make an appearance.

Chapter Twenty

Liam

The first of our guests were arriving and Kate was still to come downstairs. I couldn't leave my post by the stairs and not greet our guests, appearances were everything after all, and it would be crass of me to be absent. I tapped the toe of my highly-polished Gucci black shoes in annoyance. Paula Clarkson sashayed through the open front doors, fuchsia pink lips set in a thin line. Paula had chosen Armani tonight, and she wore it well. The dress hugged at her curves and dipped low between her breasts. The split at the front stopped just short of trashy. Her arm was linked through John Templeton's in a casual, yet dominant manner. Someone had had a disagreement on the journey here. With the amount of Botox injected into Paula's face, it was her mannerisms that now gave her away, rather than the usual facial expressions.

"Why Paula, you look lovely tonight." I leaned forward and air kissed both her cheeks. "John." I took John's hand, it was a weak handshake. John's fingers hardly curled round my hand; it was very telling.

John's jaw dropped open slightly. Paula's back straightened in jealously. I turned to see Kate gliding down the stairs. She was a true vision of beauty. The long black lace dress she wore hugged her svelte figure; the lace caressed her shoulders like a lover as it scooped across her chest. The Whitby Jet heart tickled the lace. The thick heavy stone was encased in a thin strip of silver, which came together to form a cross, at the heart's centre. Swarovski crystals were strung into a choker, from which the Whitby Jet hung. Her hair was in a tight knot at the nape of her neck, pale pink kissed glossy lips were turned up in a smile; her emerald eyes sparkled with life. I moved uneasily at that smile, Chrissie was back.

"Paula, John, I must apologise for my tardiness." Kate leaned forward and air kissed Paula's stiff body. John, on the other hand, was more than eager for any excuse to get closer to Kate, as she leaned in and air kissed his cheeks.

Kate's hand snuck through my arm, and she leaned in and kissed my cheek. I tried not to pull away as her lips unexpectedly touched my flesh. "Liam and I are expecting our first child, and well, unfortunately, I have been experiencing a little sickness." Kate looked at me; she must have seen the anger in my eyes, because she threw her head back and laughed. Her laughter was like the slightest tinkling of bells. "Liam is *so* excited." She leaned into me, and I took the opportunity to squeeze hard on her arm, in warning. Kate turned and looked at me her hand rose and touched my cheek. Her eyes were full of hate and determination. I watched her as she turned back to Paula and John, a pouty yet sensuous smile on her lips. "I know we promised to keep it a secret, really, it's so difficult to keep such an exciting secret. I just know that Liam was planning to tell everyone tonight; after all, our charity is in aid of the Special Care Baby Unit at York Hospital." I could happily have flung the bitch against the wall and watched her crumple to the floor. Instead, I unwound my arm from hers and placed a firm hand on her arm.

"Yes, of course, I was just waiting for everyone to gather first," I muttered. A thin smile played across my lips. Kate laughed again, the effect she was having on John was hypnotic as he stared at her with puppy eyes.

Paula looked less than impressed. However, the news that Kate was expecting seemed to allow the stiffness to ease from her shoulders. From this one act, I took it that John had about as much interest in procreating as I did. Paula grabbed at John's arm and all but pulled him away.

Tammy Sinclair stumbled into the room, having misjudged the last step into the house. To add to the disaster, her heel caught the hem of her powder blue dress and she went tumbling forward, her left breast making an appearance. Kate moved quickly and with ease caught Tammy; with a few quick movements Kate had Tammy's dress back up and in place, the exposed breast back where it belonged. Tammy gave a giggle, as Jeremy's arms went around his wife's waist, helping Kate to keep her on her feet.

"Sorry," Jeremy muttered as he got Tammy under some control.

I stepped forward and air kissed Tammy's cheeks, "It's good to see you Tammy." Tammy giggled again. I signalled to one of the waiters carrying a silver tray of champagne. Jeremy looked pained as the waiter came over and Tammy reached out a greedy hand.

"The roulette wheel is spinning," Kate suggested to Jeremy and he nodded his head, pulling Tammy along, making their way to the marquee where the temporary casino was bursting to life. Tony Carlton followed Tammy and Jeremy, with Jane Henderson on his arm. My nose wrinkled at the very thought of the overbearing woman being here, still if Tony wanted sloppy seconds he could have them. I just wished that he hadn't brought the trash to my door.

Tony quite fancied himself as the next James Bond, but the black tux he wore and the buxom redhead on his arm failed to impress. Jane had more flesh on show than ever before; her golden sequined dress fell away from her shoulders exposing the flesh down her back to the base of her spine. The slits in the dress showed off lean legs, if a little dimpled with cellulite. The split at the centre of the dress was that high it shouted out trash. Jane's breasts were virtually on show, and they weren't nice to look upon. Had the woman never heard of a bra; they certainly could have done with a little lifting.

I sighed as I greeted the rest of our guests. I had sold over a thousand tickets, and at two grand a pop, I was set to make more money for my chosen charity, than any of the others had been able to raise from their events. All proceeds from tonight's gambling would go to the charity, and from the bulging wallets and purses on show, my guests were set to lose a fortune. Apart from Jane, they could all afford it.

Jenny was the last to come through the door. She looked radiant in a pale ivory beaded dress that accentuated her slimming waist. Unlike most of our guests, I was pleased to see that Jenny's dress had a high neck line, and that unlike Jane she was wearing a bra. Her hair was sleek and tidy and fell to her jaw line. She had obviously been to the hairstylist today; a part of me was grateful for the effort she had made. I could not allow my sister to be less than perfect when on display at such an event. Denis pulled at the black bow tie. His suit was well cut and while the man fidgeted with it, it still managed to look good on him. That's the difference between true quality and the high street.

"Sorry we're late, Elsie wouldn't settle." Jenny engulfed Kate into a warm embrace. "You look magnificent." Jenny leaned back taking in Kate's dress and hair, their hands still clasped together. "The drums have been beating and I hear that you've been keeping a secret."

Before Kate could answer I pulled their hands apart.

"Yes, well, there's more than enough time to discuss babies. Kate, our guests are waiting."

Jenny gave Kate a wink and took Denis's arm. Denis gave a quick nod of his head at me, before turning his attention to Kate. "Great news, Kate," was the only thing he said as he walked past.

This was not Denis's scene. He was much more comfortable with his nose stuck in a book, marking papers in his study, or at work giving lectures. Why Jenny had married him was beyond my understanding. Denis was a plain ordinary man, with a messy appearance and no style; his job was neither interesting to me, nor brought in the money required for high living. Jenny had married beneath herself, and had taken a step closer to the trash that was middle class. My lips curled with displeasure at the thought. Jenny had had her time; maybe it was time for Denis to meet his maker. I'd get in touch with Jeff Green at the end of the month about arranging another accident. It was about time that Jenny started mixing with the right people.

I took Kate's arm and steered her to the marquee. I could tell from the confident way that her body swayed that she was more than pleased with her performance; had I not been so mad, maybe I could have appreciated her scheming.

The marquee covered the wide expanse of the back lawn, chandeliers hung from the metal posts. The red tiled carpeted flooring added to the luxurious surroundings. The cost of tonight's event was exorbitant. Still, from the way that everyone was gasping in wonder and envy, it was all worth it.

They would be talking about this event for some time.

The tables were all full and screams of excitement could be heard over the top of the jazz band that played on the stage to the right corner of the marquee. Champagne flowed and silver trays covered with fine food bites were passed among the guests.

The press had been invited, and cameras flashed, and notes were being taken. I'd given them the old 'it's an honour to support such a worthy cause' speech, earlier. Kate had not wasted the opportunity to tell them about our own impending baby. I had wanted to shut the bitch up, and told myself that later would have to be good enough.

The press had loved Kate's news, and I smiled secretly to myself; the bitch had thought she had won. Had she never heard of a little thing called a miscarriage?

I sighed as the reporter came over to me. "We're just about to leave." The man wore a poor excuse for a suit, and I nodded my head, taking his hand and giving it a good shake. "It was good of you to come." I watched in relief as he left with the photographer, who was dressed in jeans. *Jeans,* the man had no class.

A representative from the hospital was here, and I nodded my head in her direction. You could spot her a mile off, with her high street black dress that hung off her shoulders with little style. She waved a hand in my direction. I turned and walked over to the roulette wheel, where Tammy was sloshing champagne over everything. Jeremy had an arm around her waist, keeping her on the stool. I'd give her another hour and she'd be passed out on the floor, in a corner of the marquee. Jeremy was eyeing up the woman from the hospital, and I wondered how low some people could go. That was when I caught sight of Tony Carlton's hands gliding up the split in Jane's dress; her back was pressed hard against him.

A shout came from the front of the house and I turned to see Henry Henderson's large form coming through the marquee. He was breathing heavy as he entered. His eyes virtually left their sockets as he saw Jane getting it on with Tony.

"Jane?" Henry seemed to fade before me. He wore a pair of shabby trousers and a thick cotton shirt. His hair looked as though it hadn't been washed since Jamie had died. That said, for once the clothes he wore matched his size, and while they were made from cheap cloth, they did fit.

"Get stuffed, Henry." Jane managed to detangle herself from Tony long enough to look at her husband. Her voice grated on me. Worse still, everyone was starting to give them their attention.

"Why, Jane?" The man sounded broken. I saw Kate's eyes swing Henry's way, she felt sorry for the overweight blob, that was now well on his way to spoiling my charity event.

"I would have thought it was obvious. You promised me that you'd never let anything happen to Jamie, and then you lost all our money. Jamie would be alive if it weren't for you. Now do you get it?" Jane turned her back on Henry and wrapped her arms around Tony. Henry looked as though he was going to crumple on the spot. I looked around for the security I'd hired to keep the riffraff out; they weren't doing a good job. I would ensure that someone got the sack for this. I'd used this company satisfactorily on many occasions, tonight they had let me down, and someone was going to pay for the ugly performance that was the Henderson's. I would also speak to Tony about leaving the trash at home; if he wanted to slum it that was fine, but this was the last time he would be bringing it to my door.

Chapter Twenty-One

Kate

I watched with horror as Henry burst through the opening of the marquee, Liam wouldn't be happy about this. I didn't have any liking for Jane. The way she was treating Henry was deplorable. Jane had yet to realise that they had both lost Jamie, *not* just her. It was easy to see who had been the one giving all the love in their marriage. I was beginning to wonder if Jane had any love in her heart.

I stepped forward as Jane turned her back on her husband and started playing *let's-lick-your-tonsils* with Tony. Really, Tony should have known better than to bring Jane here.

"Henry," I coaxed as I gently laid an arm across his shoulders. The contact seemed to shake him out of his reverie. "Come; let's go somewhere quiet. You don't want to be here." I led him out of the marquee; Henry never said a word. It's hard to talk when your heart is breaking into tiny pieces.

I guided Henry into the sitting room at the front of the house. It was the furthest place we had away from the marquee. A man in a white shirt and florescent armband came forward, and I shook him away with a small shake of my head.

Jake appeared at my side as I walked into the house. He was dressed in a pair of loose-fitting caramel trousers, and even though the temperature outside was still on the warm side he wore a dark green sweater.

In silence, we walked across the marble floor, my shoes clicked out a slow steady beat as me moved. I was more than a little relieved when we walked into the sitting room and my heels were muffled by the carpet.

The living room caught the last of the summer sun. Shadows were starting to appear along the walls and floor. I didn't stop to turn on a light; instead, I guided Henry over to the plush Boston sofa, with its sea blue feather cushions, wooden legs, and gold castors.

Jake stopped at the other side of the sofa, but made no move to sit down. I perched on the end of the sofa taking Henry with me. I still had my arm around his shoulders. He needed the comfort.

"She's right, you know; I killed our son." My heart squeezed tight against my chest at his words. I looked across at Jake; our eyes met in understanding. Liam was a bastard.

"No Henry, you didn't. Jamie would have died no matter how much money you had. Jane is just hurting. I'm sure that when she calms down, she'll see that you had nothing to do with the death of your son." I wasn't so sure Jane would come around to understanding that the death of their son was an inevitable event, I wasn't even sure that there would be anything to go back to.

"Henry," I urged. He looked up, and I almost wished he hadn't. The pain that haunted his eyes was difficult to see, especially as I knew that Liam had put it there. I believed what I'd said to Henry; the death of their son was an inevitable event. The poor kid had had a very serious heart condition; all the money in the world couldn't fix it. Jane blamed the loss of their son on their lack of money. I wondered if Henry still had his money, if it would have made Jane feel differently. Money or not, something's just couldn't be fixed with a fist full of paper containing the Queens head. Had Liam not been hell bent on destroying Henry, then maybe Jane wouldn't pile all the blame at Henry's feet, and they could have found a way through this together.

Henry let out a sob. Jake moved forward handing me a box of tissues and I passed them to Henry, as he sobbed about what he had done, and how he had lost it all. Sweat licked at his skin and his colouring took on a sickly look.

"Henry," I pushed at Henry's shoulders, but it was a bit like trying to move a mountain. Henry's eyes seemed to bulge, and with shaking hands he reached for his chest.

I looked at Jake for help. Henry fell to the floor taking me with him. We landed in a tangled mess on the carpet, Henry's arms flaying around him, his body convulsing. Jake pulled me from Henry before his flying arms could hit me. I wanted to yell at Jake to see to Henry, and leave me alone.

I came to my knees, noticing that Jake had a phone plastered to his ear and was listening intensely at what the person on the other end was saying. Time slowed down, and still there wasn't anything Jake, or I could do to stop what was about to happen. The sound of an ambulance cut through the room, and the flashing blue of lights filled the room. Two men ran in. It was all just too late. They wheeled Henry out of the house and into the ambulance, I knew with absolute certainty Henry would die before they reached the hospital. Henry's world had splintered into a mass of tiny pieces, and sometimes a person couldn't live in the world that was left. Death seemed the easy option, and Henry's body was willing to provide the solution to his problems.

"You know Jake, I just don't understand Liam, why he wanted to break Henry the way he did, I don't know. What type of person would revel in the destruction of another?" Without thought my hand rested on my belly.

Jake looked at me. He rested a snarled hand on mine, where it lay on my belly. "I've watched for so long, watched the changes that made him what he is today, and still lass, I have no answers for you. But know this, you don't need to worry about that baby you're carrying. I will ensure that Liam does nothing to hurt it. Will you be able to love it?"

I looked into Jake's eyes; they showed a lifetime of regret. "My fight for my baby has already started." I thought about Liam and the anger that lurked behind those sharp blue eyes. He would get me back for my performance tonight. I wasn't so sure that Jake would be able to stop him. "I couldn't kill my baby, no matter how he or she was made. It's not their fault. While I would never have chosen to have Liam's baby, life is life and this baby is still a part of me. Jake, I will be able to love my baby, because it will never be Liam's, I'll make sure of that."

Jake nodded his head, and we stood and watched the ambulance leave, our faces bathed in blue lights.

I turned and walked back into the house as the ambulance disappeared down the road. "Someone should tell Jane," I said to Jake as we walked back toward the marquee.

Jake gave my hand a squeeze at the opening of the marquee. Darkness had come and Jake disappeared into its depth. With a deep breath, I walked inside. The noise that had been a gentle tease earlier as we'd stood and watched the ambulance carry Henry away, now shouted around me. A part of me hated the happy shouts and laughter that rang out. No one seemed to care about Henry, and I dare say that none of them cared about each other. Liam sent me a questioning look, a champagne flute dangled from his hand.

"Henry has had a heart attack. I don't think he's going to make it." I caught the smile of satisfaction that fell upon Liam's lips, before he could hide it. Sadness filled me; it would be so easy to be like Liam, to hit him until that smile fell from his lips. But I was better than that. Liam lived in a cold world; he never saw the beauty in it; never really wanted to be part of the warmth that loving someone could bring. I walked away from him.

Jane was downing a glass of champagne, and greedily reaching for another one as I approached her. She raised an eyebrow in mock salute as she poured the contents of the champagne down her neck. Tony was nowhere to be seen. That was *love-and-leave-them* Tony.

"Henry's had a heart attack." Jane looked at me, as though I had suddenly grown an extra head.

"So?" I closed my eyes and breathed deep at Jane's response.

"Jane, I don't think Henry is going to survive it."

"Quite fitting then isn't it." How cold could someone be?

"Jane, I know you're hurting right now, but think about this. You may never get another chance to talk to Henry."

Jane reached for another glass of champagne. "Like I care."

"Maybe you don't right now, but at some point, you might, and for that alone, I think it might be worth you saying your goodbyes." I didn't think that Jane would get there in time to say what she needed to, but I was not a medical expert. That had been one hell of a heart attack to me. Even if Jane never made it on time, at least she would be able to draw some comfort from the fact that she had tried.

Jane gave me a long look. I could see the moment my words penetrated her thick skull. I laid a hand on her arm. "Come on, I'll take you to the hospital." Being pregnant meant no drinking for me. I was taking this pregnancy seriously.

I led Jane out of the marquee. Jenny sent me a questioning look. I'd give her a ring later.

Our heels clicked on the cold marble floor as together Jane and I made our way through the house. Jake had already got Jake Junior to bring the Bentley round to the front of the house. "Would you like me to drive, Mrs Thornton?"

"That would be good of you, if you don't mind." Jake Junior was already opening the back door of the Bentley, and I sent a grateful smile his way.

Not everything in Liam's life was as cold as he was.

Jane settled herself into the back seat. She raised a hand as I went to follow her. "I want to be on my own." I nodded my head and stepped away from the car.

Jake Junior ran around the other side and settled himself into the driver's seat. I watched as the car travelled down the drive. I raised my eyes to the sky; stars twinkled down at me, the full moon bright in the night sky. Silently, I walked back towards the marquee and our guests. It was for the best that Jane had gone on her own. Liam would have flipped if I'd left.

Jenny stood in the hall near the stairs, concern causing wrinkles to line her forehead. I walked towards her. She opened up her arms and I leaned into them, tears threatening to spill down my cheeks.

Jenny hugged me until she felt me get control of myself. "Better?"

I nodded my head. "You're the best, Jenny."

"And don't you forget it." I laughed at her and she threaded her arm through mine. "Come on Kate, there's orange juice to be drunk, and you do look as though you could do with a good stiff orange juice, I'll even get them to leave the bits in for you." I don't think I could have gone back into that marquee if it hadn't been for Jenny.

Chapter Twenty-Two

Liam

I looked round the marquee. All was now quiet. The wheels had finished spinning and the champagne had stopped flowing; the last of the guests had left an hour ago. I looked at my watch – it was four a.m. Despite Henry Henderson's sudden and irksome appearance, the night had gone well, even better, since I would no longer have to experience another visit by the overweight excuse of a man. I had been informed that Henry had died on his way to the hospital. I couldn't stop the smile of gratification that fell upon my lips.

Kate walked through the marquee; there was a sadness about her. Henry's death had put it there, and that made me angry, because she was mine, not his to inflict emotion upon.

"I'm going to bed. I take it you don't need me for anything else."

I looked down at the green velvet of the blackjack table. "You thought you were very clever tonight, telling everyone about the baby." I heard her as she sighed out her tiredness. It was her own fault; she should have kept it to herself, and got rid of it like I'd told her to. If she was going to play these games with me, then she had better get used to the consequences of her actions.

"No Liam, I wasn't being clever, I was protecting my baby." I looked up at her, her eyes shone with hate as she looked at me, like a lioness watching its enemy sneak ever closer to her cubs. Kate didn't know how beautiful she looked as she stood there in the black lace figure hugging dress; green fire lighting her eyes. It would be my pleasure to show her exactly what I thought of tonight's performance. She owed me for what she had done. And once I was done, there would be no baby to protect.

Kate turned to go. "Where do you think, you're going?" I didn't bother to hide the anger from my voice.

"I'm going to bed Liam." She didn't turn around, which made my blood boil over.

In a few short paces, I'd caught her up and wound my fingers tightly on her arm. She turned around, eyes wide, and a little bit of fear shimmered within the depth of her green eyes. I wasn't stupid, that fear wasn't for me; it was for that thing that she carried within her belly. It was like a parasite sucking away at her body, taking its nutrients from her, selfishly and without thought. Her body would change, and whether I grew tired of it or not, she had no right to no longer be the beautiful svelte creature that stood before me now. I had forgiven her, her background, willing to overlook it because of the unusual exotic creature that she was, her beauty not only came from the outside but also within, *and* I had made it *mine*. I would not let another claim it, and that baby would take her away from me again. I would not, could not allow that thing inside her to live.

"You don't go until I say you can."

"Let go of her, Liam." Jake's gravelled voice filled the marquee, and I released Kate's arm in surprise. "Go to bed lass, you'll find that the lock has been replaced on your bedroom door. I suggest you use it." Kate nodded at Jake and left.

"Don't interfere old man, this is between me and my wife." Jake had never interfered in my business before, and it unnerved me a little that he was now. My heart went cold; I would have to do something about this, because if Jake interfered once, then he would do it again.

"Liam, that isn't your wife." My eyes widened. Just what had the bitch been telling him? It also raised the question of whom else she had been talking to. Obviously, the threat I'd made of having her husband and child killed hadn't been enough. The stupid bitch, did she not realise I had been serious? Well, she would soon find out. I slammed my fist onto the blackjack table.

"Again, old man, I'll ask you not to interfere." Jake moved closer into the marquee. I stayed where I was as I watched his old bones creak their way across the floor.

"I've watched you destroy everything, lad. I've never said a thing, but that child that that poor lass is carrying deserves to live. It quite possibly could be your own salvation."

I raised my eyebrows at him. "I don't need saving Jake, what I need is for you to go back to tending the garden and leave me alone."

Jake had come to a stop in front of me. "You think because my body is failing, that my mind has gone as well. These eyes see everything. I've known since you brought that poor lass home, that she wasn't Kate." I looked at Jake in surprise, so the bitch hadn't been talking after all; still, I couldn't see how he could have possibly known that I had replaced Kate with her twin sister.

"I haven't got a clue what you're talking about. It sounds more like the mumblings of an old brain, which has stopped working properly."

Jake drew himself as straight as his arthritic body would allow him to. He pulled out a piece of paper from the pocket hidden beneath his green jumper. Slapping it on the table he looked at me. "Don't play your games with me lad, I know the truth."

The skin along my cheeks pulled as the muscle under my jawline tightened. I picked up the photograph that Jake had slammed down. I looked at Kate and Chrissie in their pretty dresses, so alike, and yet so very different. I could tell them apart, even though they looked like a mirror image of the other. It was the eyes that separated them. In them the differences in their personalities shone.

"Where did you get this?" I looked at Jake. I could no longer pretend.

"Kate gave it to me, a long time ago; she was scared that if you ever found out you would use it against her." Kate wasn't as docile as I had thought she was. "I watched you as you dominated and tried to break that lass, watched you until the spark of happiness died in her eyes. I won't stand by and watch you do the same thing to her sister. You leave that poor girl and her baby alone. If I were you, I would be grateful that she is prepared to love that baby of yours."

Anger simmered inside me. How had this happened? I'd had it all; even when Kate had told me she was dying I had found a way around it. I would not fail; failure was for the likes of the Henry Henderson's of this world.

I walked passed Jake, our arms touching slightly as I moved past. "You have no idea what you have just done, old man."

Jake snorted. "I know exactly what I have done, and what I am willing to do to protect that baby of yours. The choice is yours Liam, take the time to contemplate the life that grows in that lass's belly. It could change you, make you more of a person."

The old man didn't get it. I didn't want to change. I liked the person I had become.

I didn't respond. I kept on walking.

Tomorrow, or rather later today, I would contact Jeff Green; it was about time that I showed Jake just what I was willing to do, and how far I was willing to go. First on my list was Chrissie's husband, Simon. I'd leave her daughter orphaned, with no hope of adoption; I'd make sure of it. Second, I would arrange for Jake to meet his maker, if you believed in that type of thing. I didn't.

Chapter Twenty-Three

Liam

I walked out the front door, the red Ferrari glistened in the sun. It had been my '*bonus*' purchase when Henry had signed the contract. Now, as she gleamed in the sun, her blood red body beckoning to me, she took on another meaning, because when I opened up her engine and let it roar out its eagerness, I would come home to find Jake dead.

I had contacted Jeff Green and put out the hit on Jake. I wanted it done while I wasn't around. The old man had been the only thing I had ever really loved. I now knew after last night that I couldn't afford such luxuries.

Chrissie's husband, Simon, was due to meet an unfortunate end later in the week; it fitted better with the man's schedule to leave it until Wednesday. I wanted to ensure that his death hit the front page of the local paper. I wanted Chrissie to understand exactly what she was dealing with. Maybe then she would book herself into the clinic and get rid of the baby, before it became too late, and we could all return to some normality. Chrissie gone and Kate back, this time for good. My opportunity of taking care of the baby matter myself had reduced somewhat since the lock on the door had been replaced; the bitch was still locked in there now.

I walked over to the car, sliding into the leather seat. The engine thundered to life as I turned it on, eager as I was to be off. Tyres squealed as I put my foot down and drove down the drive. My decision to put out the hit on Jake had not been an easy one, and it bothered me that I had had to make that decision, still I could not afford for Jake to interfere in my business, as he had last night. I didn't understand why he had chosen to side with that bitch and her parasite of a baby. That speech about the baby being my salvation was sheer stupidity talking; I did not need saving.

I was true to myself; I took what I wanted and destroyed those I felt had the audacity to surpass their breeding, and class, or that got in my way. Most people hid their true nature. Not me, I knew what I was and liked what I saw. Some may call me evil, but I liked to think of myself as being a realist.

The scenery became a blur as I increased my speed. I took the corner a little too tight. The smell of burnt rubber drifted through the window I'd cracked open. My heart beat fast in my chest, and a smile formed on my lips as I accelerated. The Ferrari eagerly responded and flew forward, like a bullet flying free of the barrel of a gun. The engine bellowed and the tyres ate at the tarmac.

I didn't see the tractor until it was too late. I pushed down hard on the brake. At the speed, I was travelling the gap between me and the tractor wasn't sufficient. I swerved and the Ferrari squealed, rubber burning. This time I didn't smile, but gritted my teeth and I fought for control.

I lost the fight for control and the car spun 360 degrees; smoke engulfed the tyres as the rubber tread burnt away. I gripped the sterling wheel tighter, my muscles taut. Sweat lined my forehead, and trickled down my back. The impact sent me lurching forward. The car crashed into the tractor. I

151

heard the crunching of glass, the screaming of metal. Pain shot through my body. I sat there semi-conscious, wondering what had happened. It never occurred to me that I may not survive this.

I heard the tread of boots; relief flooded my body. I managed to tilt my head slightly toward the noise of footsteps. A man's head appeared to my right, as the man leaned in.

"You don't look so good Mr Thornton." I looked the man over. I couldn't ever recall seeing him before, yet clearly, he knew me. Dark brown almost black eyes stared at me; his head was bald, which accentuated the harsh features of his sharp jutting jawline. The broadness of his shoulders told me that he was a tall man. Muscle bulged across his arms, a man that liked to work with weights. His clothes were high street, black jeans and a white t-shirt. No, I couldn't imagine ever having anything to do with this man.

It confused me that he would know me. Still, I wasn't about to be discourteous to him. He was, after all the only one around that could help me. "I've crashed my car." I hated it when people stated the obvious. My head hurt, and I was slowly losing feeling in my legs and arms. I could forgive myself for being obvious.

"Yeah, I can see that." The man bent down, his legs clicked as they bent. "You're dying, Mr Thornton."

My eyes widened in fear. I didn't want to die. I had far too much to do. I hadn't put out the hit on Denis yet. Kate was still pregnant. I still needed to view my position on Pete Townsend; did I still have use for him? There was far too much for me to do. I didn't like loose ends. They were an irritation that needed stamping out.

"I thought you might appreciate a car accident. After all, it has always been a favourite of yours."

What was the man babbling about?

My breath caught in the back of my throat. "Jeff Green?"

152

"In the flesh, Mr Thornton. I wanted to meet you before you died, it seemed only right. After all, you've brought a lot of business my way over the years."

My brows knitted together, I was unable to understand what was going on; why was Jeff here? I paid the man well, had never been late on a payment, something was off.

"Why?" I'd always found it strange how a three-letter word could carry so much weight.

"Simple, Mr Thornton. You put out a hit on the wrong man."

"Simon Sanders?" I didn't understand. How did Simon Sanders and Jeff Green know each other? What was their connection?

"Nope, Jake McCloud." Jeff's voice had a rasp to it, like he had spent his life chewing on sandpaper.

"Jake, *Jake put out a hit on me?*" I couldn't believe it; how could he afford it.

"Nope." Jeff grinned at my confusion, revealing white even teeth. "Jake saved my family and me from a house fire forty years ago. I owe him my life, and that of my family's. That kind of thing a man never forgets."

Sweat lined my skin. I was going to die.

I didn't want to die.

I licked my shaking lips. "Look, I didn't know. How about we just forget about the hit on Jake? I'm sure that we can come to some arrangement. Keep the money for the inconvenience."

Jeff shook his head. "Sorry Mr Thornton, no can do. You're bleeding out, by now you'll have lost feeling in your arms and legs; your heart is pumping out your blood into the furnishing of that flashy car of yours. You must be feeling real tired, bet you'd like to close your eyes."

"No, I can't die." But Jeff was right, my eyelids were getting heavier and it was difficult to concentrate, to focus on the real issue here. "What about Simon Sanders?" I needed to know that Chrissie would still lose her husband, I wanted her to suffer. She deserved to.

"Sorry Mr Thornton, I don't take money from a dead man, and as you haven't paid yet...I'm sure you can understand my position." Jeff rose, his legs clicking back in place.

"*No...*" Darkness pulled at me, and I was starting to feel so cold, so very cold.

I could hear Jeff whistling as he walked away, and in the dim recesses of my mind I began to wonder if this was really it. Was there such a thing as an afterlife? I'd never really believed in God, or the inner makings of a man that people referred to as a soul. Now, as my life slipped away, I wanted to know that this wouldn't be the end, that in some way I would survive this.

Born again, into a new life? I didn't care; I just didn't want this to be the end.

Panic filled me, and briefly my eyes flew open, I was alone, I didn't want to die alone. But then we don't always get what we want.

Today had turned out to be the worse. Jake was alive, Simon would get to live, Jenny would live out her days happily married to someone beneath her breeding, and Chrissie was still pregnant.

I'd had bad days before, but this one, this one had to be the worse.

I felt my eyelids close, and my breath shuddered in my chest.

There was no coming back from this.

I wondered if I would see Kate, meet her in whatever place she had gone to when she'd died. It would seem that we were both destined to die too young.

Chapter Twenty-Four

Jessica

I screamed out.

Sweat lined my forehead and my breath came if gasps. The pain subsided for a brief second, and I breathed in ready for the next wave of contractions to hit. I'd been at this for ten hours now, and while I knew that wasn't a particularly long time in giving birth, it felt like an eternity to me right now. The knowledge that I'd have this to do again way too soon, was not a happy thought. Miracles weren't meant to be given lightly, and my little miracles wanted out, probably about as much as I wanted them out.

"One more push," Charles encouraged me.

I didn't have time to respond, which was just as well. He was trying to be encouraging; I knew that. I found his upbeat mood condescending; after all, he wasn't the one doing the pushing here.

Another contraction hit me.

I was beginning to question my need for a home birth. Maybe that thought was way too late considering my first baby was nearly out. Everyone had questioned my decision for a home birth, had wasted their time trying to get me to change my mind. I was not a stubborn person, and yet in this matter I wouldn't be swayed. I'd received the talk about twins and complications, and so on. I had stuck to my plan. Charles wouldn't let anything happen to me or our babies, I was confident in that.

It had been important to me that my babies' first breath of air was in the place where Charles and I had first been allowed to love each other, to be together. I was a romantic, always had been. I saw no need to change now.

I was fit and healthy, Charles was a doctor. All-be-it a doctor in a completely different sector than child birth, but a doctor was a doctor. The human anatomy didn't change, just the circumstance. Not that I mentioned this to Charles, his eyebrows would have hit his hairline. I had a very simplistic view of medicine and their practices. Maybe that was the problem with the whole medical profession; they over complicated things. Not that I was going to share that view with Charles either.

A baby cried and I sagged back in relief.

"She's gorgeous, look Jess." Charles handed me the still bloodied baby.

My eyes filled with tears, and I smiled arms out stretched. "We made this." I looked at Charles and saw love and wonder shinning in the depth of his hazel eyes. The baby stopped crying and screwed up her face.

"She has your nose."

"God help her," Charles chuckled.

"I like your nose," I pouted.

The other thing I had been adamant about was not knowing the sex of our babies. I liked surprises. It just seemed part of the whole pregnancy experience to me. It also meant that as I didn't want to know, that Charles never got to know either.

My pregnancy had taken us both on a ride of surprises. First finding out I was pregnant, and then finding out I was having twins. Pain began to build again, and I quickly passed our daughter to her daddy. I smiled at the thought.

Pain engulfed me and I screamed again, and again. Our daughter cried with her mummy. This time things happened a lot quicker and in twenty minutes another cry lit the early morning rise of the sun. "It's a boy."

Charles placed both babies in my arms, and I cried in wonder and love. Honestly, I just couldn't have imagined the overwhelming emotions that hit me. Tears rolled down my cheeks. I was completely happy, and completely in love with my babies, and the man who had helped me create them. Soft lips kissed my sweaty forehead. The bed gave and Charles sat next to me. We just sat there staring at our babies; love radiated from us like a tangible thing.

"We should get them washed." The midwife stood at the end of the bed.

I smiled at her; she had the best job in the world. Giving life was an amazing thing, helping that life come into the world, was incredible.

Charles picked up our daughter and the midwife took our son. "Rest," the midwife said as she moved out the room.

My arms felt cold and empty from where my babies had lain. I laid back against the pillows and smiled. I had done something truly amazing, I had given birth to the most beautiful babies I had ever seen. Of course, there was a part of me that recognised that every mother probably felt this way, but I didn't care. My babies were made from love and born into a world of love, and I recognised that not all babies were.

I woke sometime later to the hungry cry of my daughter; how I knew it was my daughter crying I couldn't tell you. Charles passed our daughter to me and she hungrily attached herself to my breast. Not to be left out our son began to cry.

Charles held onto our daughter as I juggled and rearranged them so that they could both feed happily.

Charles chuckled. "She's definitely your daughter."

I looked down at our daughter as she suckled greedily. "I don't know. Our son seems to have his dad's appetite."

Charles laughed. "Can you manage?"

I smiled up at him. "Don't worry so much, they're doing fine, and I couldn't be happier."

"I'm so proud of you." His voice was low, almost a whisper as emotions took him on a personal rollercoaster ride. His hand gently brushed the side of my face, and I leant into his cupped hand.

Had it been possible I would have reached out a hand and touched him, would have let him know how much I loved him, how happy he made me. My own emotions overtook me, and together we stared into each other's eyes, saying everything we felt.

Christine finished her meal and Charles took her and started winding her. Jacob, however, was still greedily sucking away.

I thought about my own sister, and tears prickled at the back of my eyes. "Do you think Chrissie will understand?"

Charles looked at me. "I'm sure that she would. She'd want you to be safe and happy, even if that meant that the possibility of you both being reunited could never be."

I nodded my head. "I've been doing a lot of thinking about her lately. I think it's these two that's done it."

"I know Baby, I just wish there was another way."

I smiled at Charles. "It's OK. I know there isn't. I'm just being melancholy."

Life was like that, and one day maybe we would be able to find Chrissie, one day when Liam wasn't around anymore,

I could see my sister, let her know that I loved her and how much she meant to me.

I wouldn't give up hope, hope had brought Charles to me together, and given me two beautiful babies to love. No, I wouldn't give up on hope, no matter how long I had to wait.

Chapter Twenty-Five

Chrissie

Liam was dead.

After all these months, I couldn't believe it. I still expected him to walk through the front door, to ostracise me further from the person that I was. I took a breath and placed a gentle hand over my swollen belly. The babies moved under my hand.

The funeral had been a splendid affair. I was sure that Liam would have been pleased by the turn out. Even Tammy had managed to remain sober until after the main service. The only emotion I had felt was relief. Jenny had broken down, tears rolling down her cheeks, as she leant on Denis for support. Liam hadn't deserved her love.

I had entertained Liam's so called friends for the last time. Liam's death had seemed to release Tony from his restraint and he had wasted no time in hitting on me, as the coffin was lowered into the ground. While Tony may have cut a fine feature in his expensive black suit, I hadn't been impressed. These people acted like toddlers in the skin of an adult. I needed no part of what they thought they had to offer. We had all retired to the house, its white shiny paintwork a contrast to the many black outfits of the mourners. I hadn't been so sure about some of the outfits; they had looked a little less mournful and lot more party.

When everyone had gone, and I'd stood in the living room with the shadows spreading across the plush carpeted floor, I had broken down and cried.

Not for Liam, never for him, but for a life that even now, I could never have back.

Simon was lost to me, and it hurt, it hurt so much.

I had driven to our house the day after I'd received the news about Liam's death. I had sat there watching and waiting for Simon and Imogene to come home. I had intended to go to them, to tell Simon what had happened, but as my hand had rested on my swollen belly, I knew that I couldn't. I couldn't do it to Simon. How could I ask him to not only accept another man's child but two? I had battled with myself over this issue as I sat there watching and waiting. I could give him the choice, but would it be fair of me to do so? Over time he would build a new life. He would find someone else to love. The thought struck me hard. I knew I had to let him go, no matter the cost to myself. I had been with another man, allowed that man to touch me. The fact that I hadn't wanted Liam to touch me, to rape me, didn't change what had happened. I was angry, at myself, at Liam. I should have found a way to stop him.

I had driven away, never seeing Simon or Imogene.

It was better that way.

"You OK?" Jenny came and sat down next to me. She wore a long red jumper entwined with golden thread, and a pair of black leggings. On her feet was a pair of cream knitted boot slippers. Her hair had grown to her shoulders, and framed her face in a mass of frizzy curls. I brushed a hand over my large belly, my fingers brushing the soft cream fabric of the cashmere sweater. The grey wide-legged jersey trousers hid the way that the sweater liked to shred over

161

everything. Neither of us wore any makeup. Liam would have had a fit if he could have seen the pair of us, all comfy clothed, and not a designer label in sight.

I tucked a strand of hair behind my ear. "I'm fine."

"No, you're not, I can tell."

I smiled at her. "You worry too much."

She sent me a hard look. "Someone's got to."

Jenny had been distraught by Liam's death; she had clung to me like I'd been her life line. Even when she had learned the truth, courtesy of Jake, she had stood by me. I had disagreed with what Jake had done, sometimes things were better left. I was a big one for letting people remember a loved one in a positive way. That said, it was good to be Chrissie again. I had never known how important a name was until it had been stripped from me. A person's name was a vital part of who they were. To lose it had been like losing a part of me, of my identity.

Liam had left most of his estate to me, well Kate. I had two babies to think about now, so I had accepted the money, the house, and the responsibility of what that meant. I had more responsibility than I had ever had. Liam's old life I left behind. His so-called friends had fallen away like rats running from daylight.

My first job had been to get rid of Mrs Jones. Whether I liked her or not was immaterial; she smelt badly of stale fags, and in my present condition waves of nausea hit me every time she was close, or when I happened to walk into a room she had recently vacated. If I was totally honest, I'd say that yes, a big part of giving her the heave-ho had been because I didn't like her. Liam had, and that was good enough reason for me.

Together, Jenny and I had remodelled the house, it had been our therapy. We'd taken the house from a heartless domain, and made it something quite splendid. The expensive artwork had gone, the antiquities, all auctioned off, and gone to someone who would appreciate them. It had given me a sense of satisfaction to strip away everything that Liam had cared about, and replace it with the soft homely style of love. The house was no longer soulless and it was easy to see from the photos that lined some of the walls, with Elsie's, Denis' and Jenny's image that a real family lived here. I even had a few scattered photos of Jake and Jake Junior on the side unit in the living room. They were now my family, and I had come to love them dearly.

Liam's study had become a playroom for Elsie. I'd had the walls where the small window had been taken out and patio doors put in. The room had instantly been transformed. Fairy stickers now covered bright yellow paintwork. The carpet under our feet was soft.

Jenny flopped down on the overstuffed orange sofa next to me. The sofa was littered with animal cushions. Elsie played happily with the toys that were scattered on the floor. Jake walked into the room wearing blue overalls, and Elsie screamed joyfully and leapt toward him, like a baby on a mission she crawled along the floor. As she got closer to Jake, she stopped and stood up on wobbly legs. With the confidence of knowing that Jake would protect her, she flung herself at him.

Jake's old bones were put to the test and he lurched forward, scooping the squealing child to him. Jenny and I laughed at the two of them, as Jake fought for control, trying not to drop the very wiggly child in his arms.

"Come on lass, you've got to give an old man a chance." Elsie giggled at that, as her fingers latched onto his snowy white hair.

Jenny stood up and reached over for Elsie, putting her back in the middle of the carpet and the hundreds of toys that sat there. Jenny pressed down on teddy's red paw and he began to sing. Hungrily Elsie grabbed the bear and began chewing on his ear.

"You know, she reminds /of a certain young gardener, I have, a very easily distracted gardener."

I looked at Jake. "Jake Junior spending too much time over a certain automobile?" I enquired innocently.

"You know he is," Jake grumbled as he sat down in the high-backed chair. I had bought it and others like it especially for him, allowing him to get in and out with ease. Old bones weren't meant for super soft sofas.

"It makes him happy, and what did I want with the car," I shrugged.

"Oh yes, I'll give you that lass, it certainly makes him happy. He should be out dating a girl, not lusting after a car."

"It's an Aston Martin, Jake, it deserves to be lusted after," Jenny added.

"Not when he should be cleaning the leaves off the lawn. These old bones of mine hate the damp. Winter is coming and they know it, otherwise I would pick them up myself."

I shook my head. "No, that's not Jake Junior's fault, it's mine. I asked him to leave the leaves for the hedgehogs." Jake looked at me like I had lost my mind. I sighed. "They need the leaves to insulate themselves against the cold. A tidy garden is not always a happy garden, Jake."

Jake huffed, and I knew that that was the only answer I was going to get.

The front door bell echoed down the hall.

"I wonder who that is." I went to push myself off the sofa, no mean task given my size.

"Don't bother, I'll get it." Jenny looked at her watch. "It's time for Elsie's nap anyway." Jenny, Denis and Elsie had moved in once the renovations had been completed. They had taken up residence in what we liked to call the north wing, where my old room had been. I had taken up residence in the west wing.

164

"I'd better go too. The garden won't tend itself, since I seem to be a gardener down at the moment." I laughed at Jake's retreating back.

Elsie started crying, the echoes of her screams filled the hall. "I'll get the door lass, you see to the little one."

"Thanks Jake." Elsie's cry drifted away, and I smiled to myself as I slid off the sofa onto the floor.

Sitting on the floor I started to pick up all the toys, as Jenny, Elsie and Jake left the room, placing them into the brightly painted pink toy box. The toy box was a work of art with hand-painted princesses dancing around it, and the delicate touches of the fretsaw lattice work long the bottom edges.

Footsteps echoed on the marble floor and I turned around with a handful of toys. My mouth fell open and the toys fell from my arms, scattering across the floor. Tears stung at the back of my eyes and my mouth hung open in shock and surprise. I couldn't believe she was here, *here* in the same room as me.

Before I could say anything, she fell to the floor next to me and wrapped her arms around me. We held each other as tightly as my bump would allow, and together we cried.

Kate leant back and brushed the hair from my face. "I never thought that I would see you again."

"Me neither." We clung together until our tears subsided.

Liam's death had freed us both, allowing us to be together again. I had no doubt that if Liam were looking up at us from hell; he would be having a good old rant right about now. The thought made me smile.

Kate held out her hand and helped me off the floor. Together we sat on the sofa, hands clasped together as if letting go would make this any less real. I stared at her, she looked happy and relaxed, in a thick grey Aran sweater cut to her waist and black skinny jeans, with flat knee high boots.

Her hair was brushed back in a high ponytail, highlighting high cheek bones. She was a perfect mirror image of me.

"I saw your photo in the newspaper. It was while you were at Liam's funeral. I rang Jake, and he told me what had happened. Chrissie, I'm so sorry, I didn't know he knew about you. Had I known what Liam would do, I'd never have left." Her guilt was like a cloak of sadness wrapped tightly around her.

I wouldn't let Liam do this to her.

He'd done enough to both of us.

I raised my hand to her lips. "Don't. You had a chance at happiness, and you took it. I can't blame you for that. What happened had nothing to do with you and everything to do with Liam." Kate fell into my arms, and we hugged tightly, wrapping the love we had for each other around us, until the hurt went away.

A baby's cry rang down the hall. Kate smiled. "That's Christine, she's probably wondering where I've gone." A man entered the room a screaming baby in his arms. He wore a red thick-ribbed sweater and a pair of dark blue jeans. Black hair tickled the tops of his ears, and his skin was lightly tanned. Jake appeared with another baby.

"Sorry love, Christine wasn't happy about being left out. I'm telling you, she gets more like her mother every day."

Kate snorted, holding out her arms. "You mean more like her dad."

Jake stepped forwarded, with a baby in his arms, from the light blue trousers and white t-shirt that read *'don't be fooled I'm not a cute as I look'*, Kate's second child was a boy. I couldn't stop my hand from resting on my belly, thinking of the two babies that grew inside me. Christine stopped her crying and gave me a considering look from the arms of her mother.

"Why don't you say hello to your Auntie Chrissie," Kate said as she smiled down at her daughter.

"Hello baby girl," I said. Christine smiled at me, her chubby hands clasping onto Kate's ponytail. Christine was dressed in a light pink knitted dress, her legs covered in knitted cream tights. Both babies had a thick mop of black hair and green eyes, their skin looked as though it had been kissed by the sun.

Jake lowered the baby boy into my arms. He smelt of baby powder and fresh air. "If Jake Junior's not careful and doesn't leave that car alone, I think I may have found his replacement."

Laughter filled the room, as Jake sat down in his chair.

Jenny came into the room and stopped dead on the threshold. She looked from me to Kate. "*Oh, oh, oh, Kate?*" I don't think that I had ever seen Jenny lost for words.

Kate walked to Jenny balancing Christine on her hip and gave her a hug. It seemed to release her from her trance. "I go by the name of Jessica now," Kate said as she guided an astonished Jenny into the room.

"I can't believe it." Jenny sat down on the sofa.

Jessica, I had to remember to start calling her Jessica now.

"This is Christine and Jacob." Jessica said as she sat Jenny down on the sofa next to me.

"Isn't it amazing?" I said to Jenny, eyes watery.

"It really is. I can't believe it, how?"

I nodded my head at Jake. "We all have that conniving old man in the chair over there to thank for this."

Jake looked offended. "I have no idea what you mean lass." Like hell he did.

"Well, I think we should all give a big thank you, to the conniving old man." Jenny smiled at Jake.

"Less of the old lass, the mind's still young." Jake grumbled.

Jake Junior walked into the room and stopped, as he looked from me to Jessica. *"Wow!* That water must have packed more of a punch than I thought." We laughed at him.

"Are you sure it was water you were drinking?" I asked him with a grin.

"Definitely water, I want to take my car for a spin later."

Jake snorted, and sent me a pained look. "Come on lad, as you're here, I might as well see if I can get some work out of you today." Jake Junior looked affronted but smiled at Jake.

"Charles, it's good to see you. Thank you for looking after her." Jake shuck Charles' hand as he made his way out the door; Jake Junior following. They looked just like twins in their matching blue overalls, the legs of the overall tucked into a pair of thick brown socks that came up to their calves.

The room fell silent for a while as we all took in what was happening, and how very lucky we were to all be together again.

"So, come on, tell me everything," Jenny said to Jessica.

I watched Jessica as she told us about her and Charles' plan to leave Liam, how she had felt that she had no option but to fake an illness. She told us about how scared she was of Liam; of her love for Charles, and about their home in Scotland.

I gently rocked Jacob in my arms as I listened to her talk. I thought that she was the bravest person I had ever met. Having lived with Liam for just short of a year, I knew that he would never have allowed her to leave him. Liam had threatened to have my husband and daughter killed to make me stay. I didn't think that he would have been so lenient with Charles.

"I'm sorry Jenny, it must be hard, hearing all this about Liam; he was, after all, your brother," Charles spoke softly, as he looked at Jenny.

Jenny nodded her head. "At first yes, when Jake told me about Chrissie. When I learned what he had done, I, well, I was pretty mad at him. I've come to the conclusion that my brother died long before his body did. I just can't understand why he did the things that he did. There's just no justification for it."

I gently moved the sleeping baby in my arms and squeezed Jenny's hand. "Come on, this is supposed to be a happy reunion. We should be celebrating."

"You're absolutely right." Jessica stood up. "Come on let's raid the fridge and get this party started. Is Mrs Jones still about?"

I laughed, in some ways we were very similar. "Nope, she's gone, she smelt bad and in my present state that wasn't a good thing. Besides, I don't think that she ever really liked me. Liam liked her, and that tells you everything you need to know about the woman."

Jessica sent me a sideways look. "Amongst other things." We all nodded our heads in agreement.

"I like what you've done with the place. It actually feels like a home." Jessica remarked as we walked out the room.

"We had a lot of fun doing it." Jenny nodded her head in agreement.

The past was the past, and the main thing was that we were all together again. The babies stirred in my belly. They might never have a daddy, but they would grow up happy.

I tried not to think about Simon and Imogene, but it was difficult, seeing Charles and Jessica so happy and in love.

I took a deep breath; this was a celebration, and I wouldn't let my sadness spoil it. I had to be grateful for what

I had, and compared to where I had been a few months back, I was definitely in a much happier place.

Chapter Twenty-Six

Simon

I dropped Imogene off at school, and made my way home. The wind tugged at my jacket, while the rain whipped at my face. The nights had pulled in and today would be one of those dark miserable days, where the sun never made it out. I tried to shake off the fact that the weather seemed to match my mood perfectly.

I turned down Front Street, and walked towards the house, hands tucked deep into the pockets of my jacket. Keys in hand, I unlocked and opened the front door.

Inside, the house looked the same.

It always amazed me how some things just stayed the same, never altered. Chrissie had left, and yet everything just stayed just as it was the day she had left. It was only when I got past the visual aspect, that I really felt the change. The house echoed of remembrance, of happy memories, time now lost and never to come back. It had taken me a long time to come to this conclusion, and it hurt every time I thought about never seeing her again.

I had to move on, and today was that day, no matter how hard it was going to be.

I shook out of my jacket and rested it on the radiator to dry.

I had made myself a promise to pack away Chrissie's things today. It had been over a year since she had gone missing, and I still had difficulty thinking that she was no longer here. I couldn't hide behind 'maybe's anymore, I had to face the fact that she was gone.

The house smelt of her and the walls if I listened really carefully echoed with her laughter. But that's all they were now, just memories, and they were slowly ripping me apart. I had to move on, like Chrissie had moved on.

No one seemed to know what had happened to her. The police had no answers, just statistics on how frequent these types of things happened. Apparently, everyone left in my situation felt the same, their loved one would not just get up one day and walk out the door, disappear from their lives without any reason. There was no money trail, no sightings, and no evidence to suggest that she had been taken. Her disappearance made no sense. I clung on to the hope that for whatever her reasons, she had left to make a new life for herself. I couldn't stand the thought of someone taking her, of ending such a beautiful life.

No, it was easier to think that she had left for something better, something I hadn't been able to give her, no matter how much the thought tore me apart.

I sighed, bent and took off my damp black trainers, and moved into the kitchen. The hem of my blue jeans, were wet from the rain and brushed against the cotton fabric of my socks. I'd make myself a coffee before doing anything else. I was procrastinating, something Chrissie would say I was very good at.

As the kettle boiled I thought about Imogene. This last year had been worse for her. She had grown up so quickly since Chrissie's disappearance. Imogene blamed herself, as children do, she couldn't understand why her mummy had left, so it had to be her fault. I had no answers for her. One thing I was sure about was that it had nothing to do with Imogene. I told her this constantly. That Mummy hadn't left because of her, that she had done nothing wrong; that we both loved her so much.

The doorbell rang pulling me from my melancholy.

I opened the front door and stared at the woman before me. My heart hammered in my chest as I looked at her. I knew it wasn't Chrissie, but she looked so familiar, and so like Chrissie that my heart squeezed in pain.

"Hi." She sounded uncertain, a little scared even.

I took a breath and steadied myself. "You must be Chrissie's sister." There could only be one explanation for the woman that looked so much like my wife.

"Yes." She hesitated as she looked at me. "I was wondering if I could talk to you."

I swung the door open. "Of course, come on in."

"Sorry, I know this must be a bit of a shock for you."

"It's OK." I closed the door and started for the kitchen. "I've just put the kettle on. Would you like a coffee or anything?"

The rubber soles of her trainers squeaked on the oak flooring in the hall as she followed me into the kitchen.

"A coffee would be nice."

Without thinking I reached for the mugs and began making coffee. I heated up the milk in the microwave as the kettle re-boiled, and added the coffee, topping it up with water. It wasn't until I turned to hand over the coffee that I realised what I had done. I'd made the coffee for Chrissie.

"It's OK, we drink our coffee the same." She took the mug from me. "Shall we sit down? I have a lot to tell you, and to be honest I'm not quite sure where to start."

I stood where I was, my heart hammering once again against my chest. "Is she alive?"

"Yes." Thank God, relief flooded me.

She stood there watching me, as I tried to gather myself together. Finally, I found I could move and my heart began to slow down. Pulling a chair from the pine table, I sat down.

She shook out of her coat, and I became aware that I was not being a very good host. "Sorry, I should have taken that." I stood up and reached for the coat.

"Don't worry. I'll just drape it over the chair. It's horrid out there."

She wore a pair of black bootlegged jeans. A cream silk shirt was tucked into the waistband. Her long black hair fell past her shoulders to her waist like spun silk. It was incredible how alike they were. Their eyes had the same almond shape and tilt to them. They both had the greenest eyes I had ever seen; however, her eyes were softer, less confident than Chrissie's. I'd say that visually that was the only difference between them.

"I wanted you to know that it wasn't Chrissie's fault, she never meant to leave you." She hesitated, casting her eyes down to her lap, where her hands entwined around each other in a display of nerves. "I was married to a man that, well, was very controlling, powerful and cruel. I was so unhappy and I wanted out. There was no way he was going to let me leave, so I pretended to have cancer." The shock on my face must have registered because she looked guilt stricken at what she had just confessed. "It was the only way. If I had an illness that couldn't be cured, then quite literally there was nothing Liam could do about it. So, I changed my name to Jessica Ripley and moved to Scotland. I started a new life for myself."

I watched her, stunned. She took a nervous sip at her coffee. I couldn't ever imagine being that powerless, and yet the woman in front of me obviously had felt that way. How

174

she had accomplished this didn't matter to me, what mattered was Chrissie.

Jessica raised her eyes pleadingly at me. "You have to understand, that it never occurred to me that Liam would find out about Chrissie. I didn't even know that you lived so close. But, Liam did find out, and he took Chrissie and made her his. The fact that she had amnesia from a fall helped. Trust me; I would never have left if I had thought that he would take Chrissie away from you." Tears filled her eyes, and I watched in silence as she tried to gain control.

"By the time that Chrissie's memory came back, it was too late, Liam had integrated her into his life. He threatened to have you and Imogene killed if she said anything to anyone. She had no choice but to stay. You have to understand that."

Her guilt was a physical thing and I felt for her. Was she risking everything just to be here, to be telling me this? Would this Liam chap find out and take out his vengeance on her, on Chrissie? The skin around my face tightened at the thought.

"Liam died at the end of summer. When I saw Chrissie's picture in the newspaper, I came back to York." Jessica wiped at her tears as she spoke. More took their place.

I couldn't remember seeing a photo of Chrissie in the paper, but then high society and I were not friends, and so I wouldn't really have been interested.

Still, I didn't understand. If this man was dead why hadn't Chrissie come home? Did she think that I wouldn't forgive her, or that I wouldn't be capable of understanding?

These were hard questions for me to face, but I had to ask. "Why has she not come home? Why stay away? The man's dead, she could have come home at any time."

Jessica looked uncomfortable, her hands twisted and untwisted in her lap. "It wasn't that easy for her."

"I don't understand." To me, it really was that easy.

"Simon, Liam rapidly raped her."

I stood up and began to pace. It was probably as well that this man was dead. I felt like punching him, over and over again, until he was nothing but a bloody pulp. The thought of someone doing that to Chrissie made me feel sick.

"That wouldn't have stopped me from loving her." Tears stung at the back of my eyes.

Jessica stood, taking a hesitant step forward. She touched my arm. "She didn't come back, because she was pregnant."

I walked to the window away from her, and looked out at the rain that was quickly turning the garden into a swimming pool. "I'd have still wanted her."

I heard the sound of footsteps, and turned to find Jessica sitting back down on the chair, hands wrapped around the now cold mug of coffee. "She didn't want you to feel obligated to love another man's children. Chrissie had twins a couple of months ago."

I moved back to the table, lowered myself back down and sat on the chair. I had to force myself to sit at the table opposite her, "twins?"

Jessica gave me a shy smile and nodded her head, "Two boys."

Silence fell upon us. I think she was trying to gauge how I felt. I wasn't sure about how I felt about the whole thing, so good luck to her.

"Simon, I'm not here because I think you should know. I'm here because I don't want Chrissie to be sad anymore. She's suffered badly because of me, because selfishly, I wanted to be happy. She doesn't know I'm here, and I think she'd have a fit if she did. I just wanted to know, if you could still find it in you to love her, to accept her and the boys."

I didn't know what to say. I loved Chrissie, I really did. This last year had been hell. But could I love another man's

176

children, knowing how they had been conceived? To be constantly reminded how she had been raped time and time again? I placed an elbow on the table and rubbed at my temple.

"I'm not expecting an answer from you. You've got a lot of thinking to do. But if you do decide that you want her, and the twins, then this is where she's living now." I watched her as she slid a small piece of paper towards me.

"I leave for Scotland tomorrow, and I couldn't leave without doing this. I hope you understand why." She got up and picked up her coat. "I'll see myself out."

I sat there staring at the bit of paper, tears spilling down my face, as the front door closed softly.

This wasn't just about me. It was about Imogene as well. I couldn't destroy her world twice. I had to be sure that I could accept the twins, be capable of loving them as though they were my own. Loving Chrissie had always been so easy, and the twins were a part of her.

Still, I hesitated.

I buried my head in my arms as my elbows rested on the table and sobbed.

I just wasn't sure that I could love them, and I hated myself for it.

Chapter Twenty-Seven

Chrissie

I sat on the floor in the living room, my mind drifting as I looked out the window at the snow piling up outside. It was late October, and we were gripped in another cold spell. The news channels reported it as being the coldest for sixty years; sadly, this information did not make me feel any better. Jessica, Charles and the twins had left over a week ago, and I felt their absence badly. Given the snow, I was becoming increasingly worried about them being able to make it back for Christmas. The thought of them travelling in this weather was not comforting. Selfishly, I wanted them here, with me. But it seemed like the weather had other plans.

William cried out, and I pulled myself out of my darkening thoughts. I looked down at William as he lay on the floor next to me, gurgling happily now that he had my attention again. Thomas obviously felt he was missing out and began to echo his brothers, gurgling.

"Now then you two, has Mummy been neglecting you? Bad mummy." I tickled both their bellies. They had my skin tone, and almond-shaped eyes, however the blue of their eyes were all Liam. It didn't bother me, not as I thought it would have. I was determined that these two beautiful boys would not grow up to be like Liam. I didn't think of Liam as being their father, a father was more, a lot more than biological makeup. I thought about Simon, and all the love he bestowed on Imogene, that was a father.

The living room carpet was cream, and I was beginning to think that it wasn't the most practical colour in the world for two boys, and a little girl. The sofas were a soft buttermilk colour, with gold cushions scattered on them. Again, not particularly practical, but then this was supposed to be a grown-up space.

I'd had the photos of Simon and Imogene, that Liam had given me the day he threatened to have them killed, famed and they sat on the oak unit by the far wall near the large inglenook fire place, where a log burner sat within its confines, throwing out heat.

I sniffed the air. "Wow, you two smell, come let's get you changed." I scooped them up and went upstairs. They were too young at the moment to sleep in their own room, so I had put a pair of cots in my bedroom. However, I spent time with them, changing them in their own room, so that they got used to it. I also put them down for a nap in their bedroom, while I sat in the rocking chair in the corner and watched them sleep. I'd done this with Imogene. The peace that it brought, just sitting there watching them sleep, was hard to describe, it was immense and comforting, and brought all the love I had for them to the forefront.

The room was decorated in light green and yellow, and had a definite jungle theme to it. Lions, elephants, giraffes and bears roamed along the walls. It was a little boy's bedroom, and the theme continued onto their bedding. They were both dressed in baby-grows, William wore a blue and white stripped one, while Thomas wore a blue one littered with white stars. They might look the same, but they were unique, a little person within their own right, just like their mummy and Auntie Jessica.

179

I changed Thomas first as he seemed to be the smelliest. I swear these two little monsters were already trying to compete with one another. My nose wrinkled as I removed the nappy, and Thomas laughed. "Well, I'm glad that you think it's funny." That earned me another laugh from a very happy little chap.

"Chrissie," Jenny called.

"In here," I answered as I swapped the babies round and started to clean William.

I heard the sound of footsteps on the stairs; moments later Jenny appeared, a little flustered.

I watched her with a smile as she smoothed down her hair, and pulled at her thick ribbed orange jumper. "What's got you all flustered?"

"There's a man downstairs asking for you."

I laughed at her. "It's the repairman come to look at the washing machine."

"Well, I wish all repairmen looked like this one. If I knew he was going to be that gorgeous I'd have made a little more of an effort." I looked at Jenny's blue jeans, and makeup free face, her hair framing her face in soft waves.

"At least you've had your hair done. It looks fabulous by the way."

"You think?" She twirled round so I got a three sixty look.

"Absolutely." I picked up William.

"Do you fancy putting them down for me, and I'll go see what all the fuss is about?"

"I'd put something a little less comfy on if I was you. You might regret not doing so. Did I mention he's gorgeous?" I looked down at my black yoga pants and red sweat top, my hair hung down my back unbound.

"I'll risk it."

"Your loss." Jenny shrugged as she tucked Tomas and William into their cots, and reached for a book so she could read them a story. "Again, H-O-T! And you could do with a little fun."

"H-O-T or not, I'm not interested."

"You know if I didn't love Denis, I'd have given him a go."

I shook my head smiling, and made my way downstairs and headed for the kitchen, thinking that Jenny had taken him there, as the hall was significantly void of life. I swung the kitchen door open to find Jake Junior sitting at the table perusing some landscape drawings.

"Is there a repairman in here?" I asked looking round the kitchen.

"Nope, but Jake took a chap into the living room." My brows drew up into my hairline. Why would Jake take the repairman into the living room?

Curious, I left the kitchen and walked back towards the living room. I pushed the door open slightly. Jake sat in his chair near the log burner, his snow-white hair ruffled from the hat he now held clasped in his hands. He wore a thick cable-knitted green jumper over his blue overalls, thick socked feet rested on the floor, toes buried into the thick fibres of the carpet. His brows were furrowed in concern as he looked across at the man hidden by the door.

"Jake, everything OK?" I walked into the room.

"You remember what I said lad." Jake pushed himself out of his chair. "I have landscape plans to go over, before Jake Junior gets carried away, it's only a flower bed or two that we're replacing not the whole garden."

Jake shuffled towards me. I stood rooted to the spot looking at the man that sat on one of the oversized buttermilk sofas. His hair had grown to his shoulders in this last year, and there were a few extra lines around his eyes. His mouth curved in a nervous smile as he looked at me, hands clasped in his lap resting on black jeans, his thin grey sweater stretched across the wide expanse of his chest. He looked vulnerable, and gorgeous, and everything in the world to me.

"You know where I am, if you need me." Jake touched my arm, and my eyes finally left Simon. I now understood why Jenny was in such a flap, this was no repairman but my husband.

Jake softly closed the door behind him, and I walked towards the sofa, stopping a good metre away. "Simon?" His name left my lips, more a question than a name. My heart wildly beat against my chest and tears stung the back of my eyes. I had wanted him to be here for long, and now that he was, I was scared that he wouldn't stop.

"Jessica came to see me."

"*Ahhh.*" It explained why he knew where I was, not why he was here. And I was so very, very scared to ask.

"I've been doing a lot of thinking, Chrissie." From the shadows beneath his eyes, he had been doing more thinking than sleeping.

I took a deep breath and steeled myself for what I was about to say. "It's OK, Simon, I understand, you don't need to come here to explain." If Jessica had been to see Simon, she would have told him what had happened, told him about the boys. "Jessica's heart was in the right place, but really, I understand, I don't expect you to accept me and the boys."

Simon pushed himself off the sofa and before I could respond he held be in his arms. I clung to him, breathing him in, tears fell from my eyes. I didn't want to have to face life without him; I didn't want to find the strength to accept that Simon couldn't love the boys.

"I love you so much, Chrissie, so much. This last year has been hard without you." He kissed the top of my head and I buried my head deeper into his chest. "I need to see the boys; I need to know that I can love them." I nodded my head but didn't lift it from his chest.

His arms tightened around me, and somewhere I found the strength I needed to accept that Simon was really trying here, that like me he was hoping that he would be able to accept and love the boys as his own.

I moved from his embrace and took his hand. "It's going to be OK." Simon smiled at me, and wiped the tears from my face.

"You were always the one with all the faith. In all the time, I've known you; somehow you have always made everything work." He lent down and gently brushed his lips against mine. My breath caught as our lips met. I hoped that today would be no different, that we would come through this together.

"Come on." We walked out of the living room, and up the stairs, our hands clasped together.

Jenny looked up from the rocking chair, the book she had been reading open on her lap. She put her finger to her lips as we walked in. If she wondered why I was holding the repairman's hand she didn't say anything. Quietly, she rose from the rocking chair, and walked towards me.

"Denis and Elsie will be home soon, I'd better go down and start doing something for tea." She lent in and kissed my cheek. "He'd be nuts to let you go." She squeezed my arm and left the room.

I looked at Simon, and we walked towards the cots. "This is Thomas, and this one is William," I said softly.

As if sensing there was a stranger in their room, they both opened their eyes at the same time and let out a cry. I leaned in and picked up Thomas, as I was closer to his cot. I turned to pick up William to find Simon holding him. William stopped crying and gurgled up at Simon. "Well, hello little man." William seemed to like being called little man, because he sent Simon a smile that lit up both their faces.

Simon looked at me. "Wait until Imogene finds out she has two brothers to boss about."

I couldn't say anything, so I nodded my head as tears ran down my cheeks. I had never thought I would be lucky enough to have Simon and Imogene back in my life. I'd been too scared to believe that it was possible, and yet here we were.

"Come here." Simon reached for me, and I went to him, leaning into the crook of his arm, as we held the boys in our arms. "I've been a fool, I know that now. These little chaps are a part of you. How could I not love them?"

Simon lent down and softly kissed my forehead, I couldn't speak, I just sent him a watery smile, tears flowing down my cheek as I let go of all the fear that had built up inside of me.

Miracles are a funny thing. Sometimes they take their time to materialise, but once they do, they are worth every second, hour, day, week, month, or year that you have waited for them to arrive.